ANNIHILATION

DAVID CIAN

ibooks

new york
www.ibooks.net

DISTRIBUTED BY SIMON & SCHUSTER, INC.

An Original Publication of ibooks, inc.

Distributed by Simon & Schuster, Inc.
1230 Avenue of the Americas, New York, NY 10020

ibooks, inc.
24 West 25th Street
New York, NY 10010

The ibooks, inc. World Wide Web Site Address is:
http://www.ibooks.net

The Hasbro World Wide Web Site Address is:
http://www.hasbro.com

ISBN 0–7434–7442–2
First ibooks, inc. printing November 2003
10 9 8 7 6 5 4 3 2 1

**Special thanks to Joshua Izzo,
for going above and beyond the call of duty.**

Cover art of Megatron by Dreamwave Productions
Copyright © 2003 Hasbro

Cover design by j. vita

Printed in the U.S.A.

PROLOGUE

Like many female television anchors, the woman could have been a model for Barbie, but her voice was low, almost sultry. "....You're watching WNDC, the World News Digital Cable Network. Thanks for joining us.

"After days of having communications into and out of the city of Las Vegas closely monitored and often censored by the ruling Decepticons, our news team is finally on the ground, able to broadcast a full report to the outside world. We urge you to have children leave the room, as some of what you are about to see is quite graphic. Let's go live to Isolde Holden, reporting live from Las Vegas. Isolde?"

"Thanks, Sheila," Isolde said. "Behind me, you can see what many people have feared would come to pass: another city smashed and battered due to fighting between the Autobots and the Decepticons." She turned to gesture behind her, her long, blond hair swirling in a cloud around her. "The MGM Grand is on fire, the upper levels of several casinos have completely collapsed, and the twenty-story Century Royale fell in on itself just minutes ago. Homes and businesses near the epicenter of the fighting have suffered severe damage from far-reaching shrapnel and the fire of multiple energy weapons."

On the television screen, the images accompanying the reporter's words are shaky. It's clear that the cameraman is moving about quite a bit. Men, women and children, panic-stricken, race through the burning streets as the gigantic steel forms of Autobots and Decepticons move among them, their heavy footsteps crushing cars, awnings and anything else that happens to be in the way.

An explosion sounds behind the reporter and she utters a faint shriek as pillars of flame burst from high windows. Behind the billowing black clouds of smoke, the frantically waving hands of the helpless and the dying can be seen in the final moments of their extremity. Rescue workers, those few brave enough to stay during the onslaught, try to help, only to be consumed within the inferno themselves. Glass shatters again, glittering shards flying outward in a silver spray that is almost hypnotic.

Composing herself quickly, Isolde continued, "As you know, due to an unprecedented agreement between the local, federal and world governments, Las Vegas had been temporarily ceded to the Decepticon Starscream and his allies. This decision was, of course, reached due to the fears that Las Vegas could end up a war zone like Los Angeles, where a nuclear bomb was detonated off the coast during a battle between the warring robots. It is well known that I have been a supporter of the Autobots, and I have few doubts that they did all they could to prevent the destruction of that city....but even I am hard-pressed to understand why they have chosen to defy the warnings given to them to stay out of Las Vegas until a peaceful resolution could be found.

"Prowl and Bumblebee, with the aid of the Dinobot Grimlock and other military forces, assaulted this city. And the results, as you can see, are devastating...."

The man watching the footage tries to focus on the robots causing the destruction, and to ignore the feelings in his gut that history is repeating itself and that the human casualties in Las Vegas are going to be astronomical. It is, perhaps, a necessary thing—that the world understands how much greater than humans the Transformers truly are. They are not myth or legend, or gods—though some people supposed they were similar.

They are here. And now...

Now they are not alone.

"For the moment, the fighting seems to have come to a stop," Isolde said. "The reason: the strange, and almost miraculous, return of Optimus Prime, Jazz, Bluestreak, Megatron and—apparently—many of the people who were abducted by unknown forces in Tokyo. In addition, the returning Transformers have been accompanied by beings of some type that we have never before seen. Many appear alien, with tentacles or shining crystalline bodies. Others are stranger still. And then there are the...*others*. I don't know what to call them. Yet to look upon them is to feel a power almost palpable in the air...."

On the screen, the sky splits with a resounding crack. A rift appears the size of a skyscraper and beings emerge from the opening. The Transformers, the humans, and the alien creatures. Then, after a brief pause, the others arrive. Some look like robotic humanoids, many of them much larger and more intricately designed than the Transformers. The camera shifts abruptly, displaying a dizzying view of the ground and the burning buildings, before refocusing on Isolde Holden.

In his mansion, the man watching the spliced-together report grasps his wolf-headed cane with long, lean fingers of surprising strength. A surprised gasp escapes his thin lips. Until this moment, he had believed the Transformers to be the most powerful physical beings in the universe. But these creatures are something else again....

"At this time, it is unclear where things here in Las Vegas stand. But with both factions of the Transformers here, along with these other beings, who can say what will happen next? I will continue to broadcast reports as long as I'm able, but for now, that's all we know. Sheila?"

The station returns to the anchor in New York, who appears shaken, yet determined to continue the reports. The man presses the MUTE button on the remote, having heard enough for now. The media will beat this development to death for hours, without knowing anything more than they do right now, so to continue to watch would be a waste of his time—which is a precious thing indeed.

Time is running rapidly. It is hard to say how these new creatures affect his plans, or if the Transformers will be able to overcome them—assuming they represent a threat.

He has spies throughout the city, and he will know more, quite a bit more, in the next few hours. They call themselves the "Followers," for that is what they do. As individuals, they have their own reasons for their personal obsession with the Transformers...but as a group, they follow their orders, though they don't know where those orders come from.

Of course, they come from him. Why they follow is

unimportant. What matters is that his plans are carried out.

And he has plans for the Transformers—both the Autobots and the Decepticons. And to accomplish his goal, he will have to move faster than he'd prefer. But no matter—a good leader adjusts to the situation as necessary.

With a grace that belies his advanced years, the man stands from his chair and moves toward his office. The silver cane snaps next to his left leg with a smooth motion.

There is much to do...if he is going to capture the Transformers and find out what he needs to know.

CHAPTER

ONE

There were few things Megatron loathed more than the bright blue-and-green planet called Earth. Yet, as he stood upon its soft ground once more, the light of the sun shining on his metallic face, he felt a bit like he was coming home.

The thought sickened him. He surveyed the area he could see from the position he had taken almost a hundred yards away from the Autobots, the dying aliens…and the Keepers. Beings he did, in fact, loath more than Earth. All of them were spread out on the expansive lawn of the Seven Wonders & More hotel and casino, a sprawling structure that promised a taste of every corner of the globe. Sunlight gleamed from the roofs of pagodas and pyramids, and glinted off a replica of the Taj Mahal. Stone gargoyles jutted from the top of an ancient castle wall patrolled by animatronic mannequins in suits of armor. Hot springs and geysers shot water toward the heavens to descend into a sparkling lake, and panoramic views of a fake ocean could be seen through the windows. It was a sea of mismatched architecture.

Very few humans seemed to be about, only some of those that Megatron had helped rescue from the

Keepers' world—an act not of mercy to these worthless bags of flesh, but as a way to pay back the Keepers for their lies and manipulations.

Most of the humans who had been abducted had scattered, but more were on the way. Megatron could hear the sirens of approaching rescue and police vehicles. Then his sensors detected more than just the sirens. He heard screams of fear, despair and pain. A symphony of human suffering.

Turning his attention to the city itself, Megatron saw that this peaceful patch that they had landed in was at odds with the battlezone surrounding it. Buildings were ablaze, debris had fallen into the streets, and terrified humans clogged the highways. In the air, jet fighters circled at high altitude, while military helicopters pressed in closer to the scene. Automatic weapons fire came from the south, along with the noise of crashing glass, screeching tires, and the roar of flames.

Megatron recognized the city now. Las Vegas. A city of dreamers and fools, a place of vice and crime and greed, where the glitter and glamour were little more than illusions designed to lure in those desperate enough to seek its charms. Why had the portal from the Keeper's world opened here, of all places? And what battle had been—was still being—fought?

Smoke passed across his field of vision, cleared—and then he saw them. His warriors. His Decepticons.

He looked at the Keepers, who seemed dazed and disoriented. Their physical bodies were mere shells of the massive structures they had occupied in deep space. Optimus Prime, Megatron's most hated enemy, and most unlikely of allies, had used the Matrix to threaten the destruction of all the Keepers—who were somehow linked together and could not sever their bonds. According to lore, only one designated Prime could hold the Matrix within himself; anyone else attempting it would be destroyed.

Although the Keepers were techno-organic life-forms, the part of them that was mechanical proved just as vunerable as any of their kind to the energy of the Matrix on their bodies. Their absolute destruction—along with that of all those that the Keepers had abducted for their experiments—had been imminent when the doorway back to Earth had been opened. Everyone had escaped, including the hated Keepers.

It's time to do something about that, Megatron thought. He glanced at Prime and Jazz, and registered that the Autobots were busy tending to the various alien life-forms that had come through the gate with them, and were struggling to survive in the foreign atmosphere of Earth. For some, the density of this planet was crushing, while others appeared to have no way to draw sustenance to satisfy their body's basic physiological needs.

Excellent. I do not wish to share this kill.

Scarred, scorched, and not nearly as steady on his feet as he expected to be, Megatron strode in the direction of his fellow Decepticons. He was about to command them to strike at the Keepers when Starscream, the closest, leveled his null-ray rifle at him and fired!

The beam struck Megatron squarely in the chest-plate, sending a startling array of sensations through the cracks in his damaged armor and into his vulnerable circuit centers. Agony swept through him as disruptive energies seared his internal workings, the major parts and assemblies within his chest that were the equivalent of heart and lungs to a human. He felt as if parts of him might melt into slag, while others felt brittle. The shining white, blue and crimson metal of his attacker blurred as his sensors scrambled. Still, as he dropped to his knees, Megatron managed to scoop a huge rock from the ground and heave it at Starscream's head. He heard a dull *crack* and a thud, and the beam fell away.

As his vision cleared, Megatron looked and saw that Starscream had been dazed by the unexpected blow. Now Soundwave was bringing up his weapon, a concussion blister gun—but he was pointing it at Starscream's head.

"Die for your treachery!" Soundwave shouted.

"Hold," Megatron said, knowing that it was unnecessary to raise his voice for Soundwave, whose auditory capacities far exceeded those of any other Decepticon. He could feel his internal systems resetting as he began to shake off the effects of Starscream's assault. "I want to know why he attacked me."

"Why has he done any of this?" Soundwave asked. "For power. The minute you were gone, he tried to usurp your place. He is *mad* with the need for it. Allow me to put him down, Megatron, and end this here and now."

Starscream began to laugh—a high, chortling sound that was vaguely disturbing. Hearing it, Megatron wondered if perhaps Soundwave was right. Had Starscream gone insane?

"You mean to follow *him*?" Starscream asked, rising to his feet and turning to address the Decepticons who had assembled nearby. "For *years*, we have done as he said, followed his plans, and where has it gotten us? Are we home? Have we returned to Cybertron to finish the war and claim the glory that is rightfully ours? No! We are rooted to this mudhole because of Megatron's lack of vision, his petty vendettas, and his pointless scheming."

Shaking his head, Megatron said, "Silence the fool, but do not kill him." He glanced again at the Keepers. Their heads were down, and they appeared to be...communing in some way. In their world, the Keepers had the power to teleport objects from any point in the universe to another. If they still possessed this ability, or even a vestige of it, they might be able to use it to escape before he could mount his attack on them.

"You followed me, and in one smooth motion we gained power and control unlike any you have ever seen!" Starscream bellowed as Soundwave stalked toward him. The butt of his weapon was raised, ready to be smashed against the other Decepticon's titanium skull. "Megatron has failed as your leader. Look how easily he was snatched up and taken from us. Consider what might have been done to him—and ask yourselves if this is even the *real* Megatron, and not some pale imitation."

"You traitorous slag-heap!" Megatron roared, his rage causing him to completely ignore his previous concerns about the Keepers. He spun and leapt at Starscream, moving so swiftly that he reached his rogue Aerospace Commander before Soundwave. The ground shook as Megatron's full weight smashed into Starscream. Earth-shattering *cracks* tore through the air as his fists pounded into the torso and jaw of the offending Decepticon with relentless fury. Starscream fell back beneath the onslaught, and Megatron followed, slamming him into the closest of the Seven Wonder's facades. Concrete rained down around them as the two robots burst through the wall. They crawled separately from the rubble, then rose to face each other once more, a huge gap torn open in the building's side. Casino employees, many dressed like knights, ladies and squires, scrambled to get out of the way, having hidden themselves inside the casino while the battle raged outside.

The sound of the incoming police and rescue workers became an incessant whine, and Megatron heard the squeal of brakes and the sound of running feet as they took up positions outside. The "authorities" had arrived.

"You *dare* to challenge me?" Megatron asked, his voice eerily level, despite his anger.

"You have *failed* as our leader," Starscream sneered.

A bullhorn-amplified voice sounded from outside. "Starscream, we're here to assist you! What are your orders?"

Starscream called to them, "Megatron is a threat. Treat him as such!"

This time, it was Megatron's turn to laugh. "You've fallen so low that you've allied yourself with these useless bags of flesh? You actually expect them to save you? Perhaps your destruction would only be a mercy—put you out of your insane misery."

Outside, the voices of Soundwave and many of his other, loyal Decepticons were raised in urgent words of warning, pleading to allow them to deal with this traitor and the forces he brought to bear. But Megatron ignored them. The day *he* began to fear humans would be the day he willingly relinquished command of the Decepticons. Or, as the humans liked to put it, when hell froze over and started selling snow cones.

The humans outside began firing and the first round of concussive shells slammed into Megatron, blowing off two of his fingers, blinding him in one eye and driving him backward, nearly insensible, into another wall. Fiery, armor-piercing bullets tore through his mid-section, three striking the cavities left from his wounds on the Keepers' world.

The bullets ricocheted within his body, two grazing the neural mesh by his spine, which carried commands from his brain to his body. A third pierced his weapons' targeting array.

"Stop them!" Megatron commanded, his voice slurred and sluggish.

He looked at the wall of attackers. Two dozen humans, twelve of them perched on one knee and firing from a low position, twelve aiming from behind and over the heads of the first row. This was a military formation and not one he would have expected from local law enforcement. And the way they were dressed, like a metropolitan S.W.A.T. team, but with helmets and visors and flak jackets made of materials that were clearly not of this world, showed that they had the willing assistance of a knowledgeable soldier of Cybertron. Their weapons were different, too. They looked much more like the cannons a Transformer might carry, rather than the typical weaponry of an elite—but all too human—strike force.

Soundwave and the other Decepticons laid down a wall of fire that should have blown the humans to pieces.

It didn't.

Invisible shielding deflected everything the Decepticons had to throw at the humans, but the pounding, relentless force of the attack forced them to break their tight formation and scatter. Some took up more defensible positions behind nearby buildings, while others chose the well-armored vehicles they had arrived in.

Startled by these developments, Megatron looked at Starscream with blurring vision. "What have you done?"

"Invested in the future," Starscream replied. "*My* future. These human scientists are much more intelligent and adaptable than you would ever give them credit for—provided one knows the proper way to motivate them. In a span of days, they have been able to discover ways to merge their technologies with ours....and to improve on both." Starscream gave a wide sweep of his hand in the direction of the war-torn city. "This 'devastation' you see around you—repairing the damage will be little effort. The Autobot attack to liberate my city? I knew it would only be a matter of time before it came, and I planned for it."

Megatron stalled, inwardly pushing his systems diagnostics and repair programs to their limits. "I don't understand. You wanted this?"

"I knew it was unavoidable and made the best of it. Shelters now exist underground, and with the exception of my strike forces, all the humans who were truly loyal and useful to me were moved to safety before the Autobots and their companions stepped one foot in this city. As for the others....a loss easily borne. They would have been the troublemakers, the ones who knew nothing of allegiance to a cause or to the leader of that cause."

From the assembled mass of Megatron's supporters—almost all of whom had either volunteered or been coerced into supporting Starscream when Megatron was feared gone forever—a host of Decepticon weaponry was turned on Starscream.

"It seems the loyalty swings in my direction," Megatron said. "I have only to give the order and your destruction will be assured."

"I wouldn't give that order," Starscream said. "I have strike forces in position behind the Decepticons who have chosen to revert to supporting you. Fire on me and my people will destroy them."

Megatron hesitated, then said, "Lower your weapons."

"But he—" the shocked Soundwave began.

"Do it."

The Decepticons complied.

"So, should I take that as your surrender?" Starscream asked.

"I choose, as always," Megatron said, feeling his power increasing, "to deal with my problems myself!" Drawing upon a vast, well-shielded reserve of energy that had gone untouched for so long he had almost forgotten it existed, he launched himself at Starscream with savage fury.

His hand shot out, the eight remaining fingers piercing Starscream's chest plating. Starscream cried out in pain and surprise, falling backwards and dragging Megatron down with him. The force of the fall drove his fingers even deeper into Starscream's chest, like surgical blades through flesh, as he sought to find the other Transformer's kill switch.

"I'm going to rip your spine out," Megatron hissed.

Then Starscream's legs drew up. The sole of his left

foot was positioned partially over Megatron's upper chest and face, the heel of his right digging into him at an angle.

Megatron realized what was about to happen. "No!"

It was too late. He tried to draw back, but his fingers were locked in the chest of his fellow Decepticon. Starscream's wings spread out, his burnished white and blue metallic legs trembling with power as blinding plumes of white hot fire erupted from his jet boosters, which were located in his heels. The flames burst against Megatron with the heat and strength of a star going nova.

In a blur, the pair smashed through the casino, splintering wood and tearing through steel. Megatron felt slot machines explode against his face, and chunks of concrete battered him as he was hauled through another wall and into the sunlight. Carried by the explosive thrust of Starscream's engines, the pair of entwined robots tore across earth and concrete, blasting through parked cars, and ripping along a huge expanse of highway before they reached an incline and skidded up at an angle. A renewed blast of energy from Starscream fired them high into the sky. his hands clamped over Megatron's forearms, holding him in place. Megatron dug frantically at his enemy's chestplate, determined to make good on his promise to tear free the rogue Decepticon's spine.

With violent shifts of his weight, Megatron threw Starscream's normally precise flying into chaos. They spun in midair, pirouetting and spiraling, and Megatron saw what must have been Starscream's intended destination rushing toward them.

It was a power station, far from the high-rise hotels and casinos, far from the manufactured beauty of the city's heart. Beyond a low-lying production plant, he saw a huge field the size of several city blocks. Steel towers rose up from it, topped by sharp spires crackling with strange, blue-black energies. Among them were what might have been water towers, but he suspected from the dull gleam of the dark spheres themselves—the gleam a telltale sign that they were manufactured from the same mix of Earth and other-worldly science that Starscream has used to outfit his human strike force—that they contained a substance that was neither as pure nor as powerless as water.

Starscream struggled with Megatron, striving with all his considerable strength to pry his former superior loose, but Megatron held on. He guessed that Starscream wanted to send him crashing into one of those towers—and to his doom.

Starscream's angry and increasingly frantic attempts to dislodge him became even more focused. Megatron's resolve to hang on matched these attempts erg for erg.

"If I go," he hissed, "I won't be going alone."

Cursing, Starscream tugged to one side, altering their trajectory. His wing scraped along the closest tower, and a torrent of hissing blue-black liquid energy splattered them both, sparking in angry currents along their metal bodies. It was some form of Energon-charged liquid with corrosive properties. Smoke rose from the two combatants.

The two metal titans tumbled higher into the air. Starscream struggled to change direction, apparently intent on flying them back to the power station.

"You lunatic!" Megatron warned. "You'll destroy us both for the sake of your vanity!"

Starscream said nothing, but the mad glint in his

eye, and a vague cackle warned Megatron that perhaps he had thought of another way to dislodge him in time to send him into the corrosive liquid. Which was *not* what Megatron had in mind at all.

Taking a desperate gamble, he yanked his damaged right hand from Starscream's chest and reached down to pry open a small emergency panel on his own hip. The protective plating fell away, dropping several hundred feet to the ground, which was nothing more than a brownish desert blur below them. From a long ago battle, Megatron had saved a souvenir—a small laser pistol.

As they flew toward the still sputtering water tower, Megatron took aim at the pierced sphere and attempted to fire, though he was unsure if the weapon would even function after so many millennia of neglect.

An amber beam of energy shot out of the pistol and the water tower exploded.

A cloud of black, crackling energy with an inner core of white and gold fire reached out from the center of the explosion. Its invisible waves of shock force struck the entwined robots before the clouds of corrosive fires could envelop them both.

The explosion that followed shot the strange energy over a mile into the blazing afternoon sky as the plant was consumed. A dozen more explosions followed, vaporizing everything within a ten-block radius, and a dark cloud settled over the area—a dome of acrid smoke.

Megatron and Starscream flew a dozen more miles, then descended, crashing down into the sandy wastes of the desert beyond the city. They parted, each stumbling to his feet.

Starscream looked at the dark cloud on the horizon. "A minor setback. But you've gazed upon just *one* of my works, and have now seen my power. The loss is mitigated."

"I...will...destroy you," Megatron snarled.

"You will try," Starscream replied.

Megatron surveyed this new battleground for anything that might be used as a weapon. He saw a half-dozen abandoned construction vehicles partially buried in the sand, but nothing else. Then a buzzing sounded as a trio of insects circled his metallic skull.

"No," Starscream commanded. "Get away from him."

All three insects flew away from Megatron, taking positions at points equally distant. Then they transformed. Each grew in size, their mechanical bodies clanking as they unfolded. The one closest to Megatron's good eye suddenly revealed a cobalt-blue head, a purple torso with an orange chestplate, golden shoulders leading to bulky arms, silver legs, and calves and feet of purple, crimson and blue. A single crest rose over his beady eyes as he aimed both his blaster and his head-mounted mortar in Megatron's direction.

"Bombshell," Megatron said, addressing the Insecticon. "You can't be loyal to this one."

"I'm not alone," Bombshell said.

Megatron glanced at the other two Insecticons, who had also transformed. Kickback's wings rose like blades behind his back, and his golden chestplate and antennae glowed in the harsh sunlight striking his cobalt blue body. Shrapnel was stockier, with antennae that protruded from the sides of his head like jagged tuning forks and glowing golden eyes in his deep-blue, impassive face.

Both also had their own weapons trained on Megatron.

Standing stock still, Megatron returned his gaze to Starscream. "Why did you tell Bombshell to stop? He could have taken control of my mind with his stinger, his cerebro shell. You could have ordered me to cede power to you, then destroy myself."

"That is *not* how I will attain this victory," Starscream said. "Soundwave may be fiercely loyal to you, but many of the others have simply fallen back into routine. I will show them the error of their ways."

Megatron laughed. "You won't get the chance. They are on their way here by now. They must be. And when they arrive, the four of you will be no match, not even with your human strike force. You *had* the element of surprise. By now, my forces will have already come up with a strategy to destroy all that you might bring to bear against us."

"Actually," Starscream said, "I'm far from being done with my surprises."

And with that, Starscream said a name that Megatron would never have believed he would hear as a possible enemy. Yet, even as he watched, the six abandoned construction vehicles rose out of the sand and transformed, each becoming one of the Constructicons that ultimately comprised the titan-like Decepticon called Devastator.

The truck with the shovel crunched and wailed with the sounds of straining metal as it became Scrapper, while Scavenger's long tread and power shovel were reconfigured as he took robot form. Bonecrusher, Hook, Long Haul and Mixmaster also transformed, from bulldozer, crane, carrier and concrete mixer to four more determined, and deadly, opponents. Then the six moved again, their bodies clamping and clanking as they fit themselves together, soon drawing up into the form of the towering Devastator, who took his place directly behind Starscream.

"I had the Insecticons repair Devastator after his unfortunate encounter with the Autobots and their allies," Starscream said.

Megatron nodded. "Then you're controlling him."

"I never said that," Starscream said, laughing again in his hollow, eerie way. "Your day is done, Megatron. Your dreams are no longer shared by all the Decepticons. Soon, they won't be shared by any. Only my desires will matter."

"You would abandon hope of leaving this world?" Megatron asked. He was still weakened and trying to buy time until his forces arrived—though he now wondered if his warriors could defeat this group. The task might be particularly difficult if those humans collaborating with Starscream made it here in time, though admitting that they posed a threat at all galled him.

"I would and have begun to accelerate the development of technology on this world to find a way back," Starscream said. "And when we return to Cybertron, it will be with millions of human soldiers who will be able to inflict the kind of damage you have suffered. That and more. It may take generations—it will certainly take cooperation. I don't care. I have time. All I need is to eliminate the obstacles in my path."

"The humans will never accept their roles as cannon fodder for your army," Megatron said, certain that Soundwave and the others would appear on the horizon at any time.

"Their loyalty has been well paid for," Starscream said. "They believe in my vision. They know that even if they fall in my service, all those they care about will be well provided for. They *don't* believe in your vision. How could they? You don't have one. Mine is simple: We will command two worlds, once this one is transformed and a war on Cybertron can be staged. Then, we will have a whole universe for the taking. We will win through deception, through intelligence—values you seem to have forgotten. Brute force and blind hatred will not win the day. And those are the only two qualities you have."

Megatron thought carefully on his enemy's words. Starscream's plan had merit—though it involved trusting and collaborating with the very race that should be little more than slaves to the Decepticons. Perhaps it was time for a deception of his own. He placed his sensors on full alert, hoping to gain some indication that Soundwave and the others were coming. He found nothing. What on earth was keeping them?

Humiliating though it would be, Megatron knew that he needed time. Time to get himself repaired and time to plan.

Sighing, he bowed his head. "Your words make sense, Starscream. Perhaps I have been…shortsighted in not working more with the humans." He waved an arm in the direction of the empty desert. "And, as you can see, my allies are…not so loyal after all. You have me beaten."

Starscream nodded, his arms crossed over his chest. "Go on," he said.

"I…can see that your vision is greater than mine," Megatron said. "And you were more right than you know about the damage I have taken—both here, since my return, and on the Keepers' world. But I can still be of use. Don't destroy me, Starscream—that will only create more strife. Let me serve you—as only an experienced leader can."

"*You* would serve *me*?" Starscream asked. "You would vow loyalty to me as the new leader of the Decepticons?"

Megatron nodded. "I have little choice. If I don't want to be destroyed, I must bow to the greater power. You."

Starscream laughed. "Oh, how perfect," he said. "Very well, Megatron. Seeing you grovel for your life is worth delaying your destruction. But I warn you—if you cross me, I'll have Devastator rip you limb from limb."

"I believe you," Megatron said, looking up at the gargantuan form towering over Starscream. Internally, his very circuits were revolted, but his choices were few...and revenge would be sweet when the time came. "How may I serve you, Starscream?"

"Return to the city," Starscream commanded. "You will give the oath of loyalty tonight—in front of the other Decepticons—and my rule will be cemented by your surrender."

"As you command," Megatron said, turning to go.

"One more thing," Starscream said, and Megatron turned back to face him, just in time to get a large fist in the face that sent him sprawling onto the desert floor. "Be sure and mention the new order of things to the others. I wouldn't want there to be any future misunderstandings."

Megatron climbed slowly to his feet, his mind filled

with thoughts of roasting Starscream in a river of molten lava. "As you command," he repeated.

"Good," Starscream said. "Now let's get back. I have a city to restore...and to rule."

Your time will come, Megatron thought. *I escaped the Keepers—and in time, I will destroy you.*

TWO

The silver and gold glow of the casino's lights gleamed upon Optimus Prime and Jazz. The Autobots knelt over the last few aliens who had escaped to Earth when the Keepers' world exploded—and whose lives still hung by a few spare threads as they struggled to adopt to the climate of this world and its unusual conditions.

"Optimus," Jazz said, "I've got one of those crystalline guys." Refracted light danced from his visor, though the sparkling, diamond-like body of the creature was slowly fading. "I'm not sure what to do. My third-party diagnostic and treatment routines aren't coming up with any suggestions."

"Shoot it," Prime said, his voice flat as he fastened a mask filled with toxic gases over the squid-like form of a six-armed alien. Several human rescue units had come to the scene, and the Autobots had scavenged everything they could from the vehicles as the human crews mostly stood back, silent, attempting to wrap their minds around the field of diverse creatures that had just sprung up outside the casino. The Autobots had even ripped apart the vehicles themselves, using parts from their engines, carburetors, filtration systems and more to create whatever they needed to treat the ailing beings.

"Shoot it?" Jazz repeated, not sure he had heard his friend and commander correctly. "But we agreed, no matter how bad it looked, we wouldn't—"

Prime didn't bother to repeat himself. Instead, he snatched up a laser pistol that had landed nearby, took aim, and fired into the chest of the crystalline warrior.

"Whoa!" Jazz yelled, leaping backward and almost falling. A gasp rose up from the humans Prime had rescued from the Keepers' world as a torrent of energy ripped into the crystal chest. The result was a dazzling kaleidoscope of sparks and crackling strands of energy that rose in a whirlwind from the alien's chest and then settled, the weapon's discharge racing out from the body's core to the head and extremities like blood carried through a human body. The crystalline warrior's back bowed, then he settled back, nodding happily, his glow bright once more, his chest already repairing its damage.

Prime tossed the pistol away. "Low-range yield. It's like sitting out in the sun for these guys."

"Huh," Jazz said. "That trick could come in handy."

The human watchers inched closer as the alien sat up, ambling toward three more of its kind. The humans Prime had saved numbered almost two hundred. More rescue units had arrived and were tending to the various injuries many had sustained in the literally hellish pits of lava and flame through which they'd been driven by the merciless Keepers.

The other aliens, nearly fifty in all, including specimens of several different races, fell into two, easy-to-discern, categories: Those who had already perished—victims of biochemical contagion brought on by contact with other aliens, or due to an inability to survive Earth's "normal" atmosphere and gravity—and those who *would* survive and perhaps even thrive here.

This mission of mercy had kept Prime from targeting and attempting to contain the Keepers. The lives of these aliens, and the lives of thousands more that may have been lost on the Keepers' world, were their responsibility. Prime and Jazz had not allowed themselves to become distracted by the conflict between Megatron and Starscream—though it was difficult for Prime to pick which one he *wanted* to come out on top. Even when the strangely armed humans had appeared, and Bumblee, Prowl and Grimlock had engaged the remaining Decepticon forces, they continued their work.

Apparently impervious to the climate changes, the Keepers had simply observed. They could have tried to escape. They could have attacked. Instead...nothing.

Were they waiting on him? The very idea made Prime livid.

Suppressing his emotions, he tended to the last of the aliens, another who would survive. Then he and Jazz rose and turned to confront the Keepers.

Before the Autobots could call out to the strange techno-organic creatures, two humans burst past the rescue workers.

It was Spike Witwicky—and someone Optimus Prime had never seen before. However, judging from the way the man carried himself, Prime guessed he'd seen his type on plenty of other occasions. He had "special operative" written all over him.

"Prime! We didn't know if we'd ever see you again," Spike said, his pleasure evident on his face. He quickly introduced the man with him as "Franklin."

Prime gazed down at his friend, wondering how Spike had come to be in this place, and why, in the name of all that was decent, would the police officers he had seen willingly side with the Decepticons. The presence of the operative with Spike suggested that perhaps some of the answers would soon be forthcoming.

"Who are those...guys?" Spike asked. "The ones that look like bigger versions of you—well, kind of, I guess, but not really. And why's Bluestreak with them?"

"They're the ones who took us," Prime answered gravely. "And Bluestreak...Bluestreak isn't—"

"That's not Bluestreak," Jazz interrupted swiftly. "They used his body to make that thing."

Even the man with Spike was stunned. "Bluestreak is dead?" he murmered.

"I don't believe it," Spike said.

"I was there when he fell," Jazz said. "I saw the light go out of his eyes. Whatever that *thing* is, it's not him."

"There's a lot we need to talk about," Spike said, his hand moving for something in his pocket.

The agent stopped him, his hand moving so fast that Prime could barely see it move, even with his greatly enhanced sensory apparatus.

"There'll be time for that later," Franklin urged. Spike's hand fell away from his pocket.

Prime scanned the two humans and was not surprised by the muddled readings he got back. The source of the strange information was the man standing with Spike.

An augment, Prime noted. He had read confidential reports about various governments salvaging bits and pieces of his kind who had fallen in battle to glean new insights into science with their findings. They ultimately were able to produce humans with bio-mechanical implants who could move faster, process information quicker, and recover better from injuries than ordinary mortals.

They were a fascinating and frightening group. It had taken human psychiatrists the better part of a decade to discern the right mental makeup necessary for someone that would willingly part with a piece of their humanity and not be driven insane. Even then, the candidate selection process was uncertain at best. Prime had heard that sometimes the augments would go mad for no apparent reason at all, sometimes long months or even years after being changed.

It worried Prime to see Spike in the company of such a person.

"I have to speak with them," Prime said, nodding in the direction of the Keepers.

"I'll come with you," Jazz volunteered.

"Us, too," Spike said.

Prime shook his head, remembering all too well the incredible power the Keepers had been able to wield over Autobots and Decepticons alike, as well as humans. The Keepers could control their move-ments, turning them into puppets. They could even manipulate their capitves' feelings, to the point of engendering a certain sense of awe, loyalty and kin-ship. "No," he said. "It should be only one of us to start with."

In their world, the Keepers had been dangerous beyond reckoning. What were they now?

"Only one of us," Jazz repeated solemnly. "You mean, that way, if the first of us who goes to them gets smashed like bug on a windshield, the other will be around to help evacuate everyone else."

"That sums it up," Prime said, stepping away from his fellow Autobot and crossing the distance separating him from the Keepers.

On closer examination, the hastily created bodies of the Keepers were monstrous and horrifying. They stood, two dozen strong, looking like bizarre surrealist paintings brought to some gruesome form of life. Mocking remnants or all-out parodies of humanoid bodies mixed with industrial nightmares.

Wet, writhing tentacles with metal needles in their mouths reached out from the churning masses of grinding gears, obscenely pumping pistons and rattling chains. Some were poised on giant treads, others had skeletal human or even animal feet, the bones interlaced with steel. Muscle stretched like a thin and membranous bat's wing or was thick and reinforced with metal threads amidst the gristle and fat and cylinders that made up their forms. Most had human or animal skulls jutting from their bodies, some with complete human skeletons.

A single Keeper edged out in front of the others. Gigantic spikes—covered with silver metal that flowed like mercury to cover, then reveal the ivory sheen of bone beneath—shot from its mass in every direction. A human-shaped skull, three times the size it should have been, stretched out from the top of its mass, the otherwise empty eye sockets glowing an unearthly blue-white.

Prime stared at the Keeper, thinking of those he had saved, and wondering into what fate he had delivered them....

"Optimus Prime," the Keeper said, with what might have been a laugh. "Have you come to ask our forgiveness?"

Prime shook his head. "I've come to take you into custody from crimes against humanity."

"How do you propose to do that?" Its voice was rusty metal over gravel.

"By force, if necessary."

"The time for that is past," the Keeper said, somewhat ruefully. "We were in your power. You could have destroyed us—but that would have meant accepting oblivion along with us. You wanted to live."

Prime didn't dignify the taunt with a response. The Keepers had created a world by fusing together their various techno-organic bodies, some of which had grown to the size of continents on Earth. Prime had opened his chest, withdrawn the Matrix, and forced the object, along with its near indescribable power, into the closest living wall of that world. Only one who was worthy of being Prime could contain such power. All others would be destroyed.

If Prime thought for an instant that even one Keeper could separate its consciousness from its physical form, he would have remained on that world to ensure the destruction of them all.

Now, he had unleashed upon the human race...what?

He didn't know.

The Keepers had been all-powerful in their own domain. Would it be the same here?

He had to find out.

"Am I to assume you will resist confinement?" Prime asked.

"Assume what you like."

"And all of you are of one mind about this?" Prime asked. He did his best not to look in the direction of the abomination that had been Bluestreak, his friend and fellow Autobot.

"I am The Voice. Address me and no others."

"You command the Keepers?"

"I am he who has accepted the unpleasant chore of communicating with...lower beings."

Prime's hands fell casually to his side. "Oh. Okay."

With blinding speed, he whirled, his hand closing on one of the long, blade-like protrusions jutting from the Keeper's grotesque form. It snapped off in his hand, and a high shriek of pain came from the Keeper as the monstrosity registered a sensation it had not anticipated.

Prime had no intention of letting the creature suffer. That was not his way. Instead, he whirled once more, arcing back in the direction of The Voice's skull, the shining blade in his hand. It sliced neatly through the top of the Keeper's head, creating a shower of sparks and a chorus of outrages cries from the other Keepers.

The top of the creature's head snapped violently off, careening into the air like a bottlecap tossed by a child.

This was a desperate gamble, but Prime could think of no other way to force the Keepers into acting without thinking, and thus allowing him to find out what he might otherwise not know: the limits of their power in these new bodies.

"Insolent box of bolts!" shouted one of the Keepers beside the shaking, sputtering Voice.

Yes, Prime thought, sensing their power growing, feeling them rise to his provocation. He could only hope, of course, that he would survive what would come next.

He waited, remembering the cruel punishments the Keepers had doled out on their world, the manner in which they invaded his body, and controlling it in the fashion they chose. Or they might choose to inflict myriad forms of damage and mind-rending torture, only to restore one to optimal functioning capacity just in time for another life-or-death battle for their own amusement.

He waited, and the tension eased.

"It is done," the Keeper called The Voice said, rising to what passed for its feet.

Prime wasn't all that surprised by the speed at which the creature had regained its composure and functionality. He had assumed that its brain would not be in the head, but the consciousness would be housed at the center of the heavily fortified torso. Apparently, his assumption had been correct.

When Prime didn't respond, The Voice repeated, "It is done."

Prime looked around, confused. Nothing had changed. Nothing had been done to him or the environment nearby, nor to anyone in sight. What were they talking about?

The human that Spike had identified as Franklin came running.

"Holy Mary, mother of God!" he yelled, his right hand pressed up against the side of his head as if a hornet's nest had just been disturbed in his brain. Prime could almost make out a demanding, panicked voice coming from *inside* that man.

Franklin looked up, his eyes wide. He stopped well before reaching the Keepers. "Los Angeles," he croaked, pale and out of breath.

"What about Los Angeles?" Prime asked, fearing the worst.

"It's gone," Franklin said. "Completely off the radar like it's not there." He shuddered. "It's *not there!*"

Franklin wore no external devices to suggest that he was receiving communications. In fact, he looked a bit like a lunatic hearing voices in his head. Yet Prime could trace a signal coming from…somewhere…and the operative was receiving it. That data was true.

The Voice motored forward, causing Prime and the agent to look at him with alarm. "You will deliver a message for us," it said.

Prime wished to say that they would not serve the Keepers, not even in this seemingly minor way. Instead, he kept his silence, wondering if all those who had remained in Los Angeles—even after the city's tragic tumble into chaos following the explosion of a nuclear warhead offshore during a battle between the Autobots and Decepticons—had just lost their lives.

If so, did that mean that the Keepers had spoken truly? Was there still more blood on his hands?

The Voice stared at them, the top of his skull sprouting metal fibers that rose up, knotted, and began to reform the clipped off section. "This is what you will say: 'People of Earth, we are your Keepers now. We are your rulers. We are your gods. Embrace us as such. Place your lives and your destinies in our hands. You have three days to comply. During that time, we will prove our strength to you. Submit to that strength. Failure to do so will result in the harshest of reprisals.'"

In a shower of blue-white energies, all the Keepers vanished.

Prime stared at the spot they had inhabited. They might as well have been a dream...yet their presence, and their evil, would now be felt by all mankind.

"Do we tell them?" Prime asked, considering whether or not they should be the ones to break this news, given the controversy already surrounding the Autobots and Decepticons. Worse, what would the impact be on a world already on the edge of madness?

"Considering what they just did?" Jazz asked. "I don't think we've got much choice."

From the ground, Franklin called, "I think we have other problems right now!"

Prime, Jazz and Spike turned to see what the operative was pointing at.

Heading straight for them at full speed were Bumblebee and Prowl....and behind them, a full contingent of *very* angry Decepticons.

THREE

The sun was beginning its long descent to the desert valley, casting shadows over rock outcroppings like long, dark fingers. The sprawling city of Las Vegas lay ensconced in its own neon brilliance, a mad rainbow of colors that bathed the stone walls, glass facades, streets and rippling fountains, even during the day. The city was a perpetual summons to the desperate, lost souls who cast good money after bad in the hopes of making it big.

Las Vegas. The ultimate playground for power and greed. A Decepticon paradise.

It's no wonder Starscream took it for his home base, Bumblebee thought as he raced down Las Vegas Boulevard, a few miles from the south end of what was known as the "Vegas Strip": a long road filled with more gambling halls and casinos than any other similar stretch of road on Earth. Horns blared and fists were raised in anger as he weaved in and out of traffic, even moving into the oncoming lanes when the north bound traffic grew clogged. With the chaos of the city lights and the desert night descending in its usual precipitous fashion, none of the angry motorists could see that this particular vehicle lacked passengers at which to hurl abuse—or a driver at all, for that matter.

At least, not a *human* driver.

"Prowl, man, I hope you're not somewhere gambling, because I could really use your help here," Bumblee broadcast, his sarcasm almost concealing his nervousness. He'd gone out to try and determine the locations of the remaining Decepticons and had found most of them, or at least those that mattered. Of course, they'd also found him, and at present, he had several of them hot on his tail. If he didn't meet up with Prowl, Grimlock, and the rest of their forces pretty soon, he realized that might be the shortest drive of his life.

Slashing through the heavy evening traffic, Bumblebee's sensors suddenly exploded with reports of incoming fire. Realizing he'd lost his anonymity among the glut of cars on the road, he transformed in a blur of yellow and blue into his normal, robotic form and continued racing forward without missing a step. He moved carefully, gracefully, as though dancing through a field of eggshells. Trying not to step on the cars around him took immense concentration—unfortunately, it also meant he had to slow his pace, allowing his pursuers to close the gap. He glanced over his should to see three missiles converging at supersonic speed on his position.

"Prowl!" was the only shout Bumblebee could manage as he thundered forward, three spears of death sniffing on this trail and closing in for the kill.

The "Welcome to Las Vegas" sign at the edge of the city blurred past, and he was in the city proper. Just ahead were the gambling palaces that drew so many humans to this neon-draped oasis. To the left, the opulent Mandalay Bay, the pyramidal Luxor, and the Arthurian-themed Excalibur; to the right, the Tropicana. Beyond that, to the left and right respectively, were New York, New York and the MGM Grand. The former was a three-block recreation of the East Coast city in microcosm, the latter a green-glassed, somewhat blocky edifice before which a snarling, golden lion towered. A wide metal bridge connected the two casinos across the width of the boulevard—a walkway quickly vacated as the humans on it realized the giant robot was headed their way.

A desperate plan began to form in Bumblee's mind. With his sensors blaring of imminent destruction, he raced flat out, his servomotors straining to meet his demands. At the last possible microsecond, he transformed back to vehicle mode, his tires screeching as they swept along the asphalt. He streaked down Las Vegas Boulevard, beneath the walkway. The missiles moved to strike the target—and slammed into the concrete and metal instead. The detonation was horrific, pulverizing the walkway's middle section. The shockwave sent debris flying in every direction, while the concussive blast of air shattered windows hundreds of feet in every direction.

A half-mile down to the road, Bumblebee was unharmed by the blast. Looking back at the burning wreckage, he gnashed his gears.

What the Decepticons force us to do. His cybertronic brain ached from the strain of it all. *No wonder most humans don't trust us....*

Lost for a few brief seconds, the rhythmic vibrations of an approaching robot told Bumblebee that his enemies had found him—most likely Skywarp, who was as cunning and mean, but not exceptionally bright. He'd obviously been repaired on the Nemesis by Starscream and brought back into service.

"Bumblebee, you're okay!" The voice caused him to raise his head as Prowl slid to a halt and dropped to one knee beside him. "I was getting your broadcast, but for some reason you weren't responding. Thought we'd lost you for a couple of minutes there."

Relief flooded Bumbleebee as Prowl laid a hand on his shoulder and helped him to his feet, but once more his sensors screamed of incoming fire. Both he and Prowl immediately went into defensive stances as a Decepticon streaked toward their position. Thundercracker, whose dark blue body looked almost black in the deepening night, screamed overhead at Mach 2.

Prowl jumped to one side, his ultra-sophisticated logic center immediately computing every possible flight path Thundercracker could take. Bumblebee's sensors were fed the information in nanoseconds, so he was able to adjust for the data that Prowl provided.

Calculating for the hundreds of vehicles and thousands of humans in the immediate area, and knowing the jet fighter would swing around almost immediately, Prowl quickly strode north down the street. "Bumblebee, head for cover. You've found them—now it's time that I take care of them."

Bumblebee did as he was told, finding some shelter in the shadow of a building, where he watched as Prowl's sensors strained into the night, computing probable paths and optimization of possible courses of action. Several seconds passed, then his shoulder cannons launched a brace of wire-guided missiles that flashed into the inky blackness high above the city.

A fiery explosion lit the night as the missiles found

their target, detonating against Thundercracker before he could make his second pass.

"All right, Prowl!" Bumblebee cheered.

Thundercracker's brain was momentarily scrambled by the horrific temperatures generated by Prowl's missiles, and he spiraled down out of the sky, dropping like a stone to slam into the ground in front of Caesar's Palace. The impact pulverized the statue of David, and knocked others off their pedestals, while damaging the building's façade. *He might be down for now*, Bumblebee thought, *but he's certainly not out*.

Before Prowl could respond to Bumblebee's congratulatory comment, a solid wave of sound rolled down the street, slamming cars and shattering windows, knocking people off their feet, and striking him directly in the back. Thrown down, the Autobot carved a jagged furrow in the asphalt as it crumbled and buckled around him. He didn't get up.

"Prowl!" Bumblebee yelled. He stepped forward, wanting to help his companion. The sonic blast had originated from Soundwave. Bumblebee didn't have a hope of stopping him...but he had to help Prowl. Somehow.

A sound like twin trains approaching at 80 miles an hour cut through the night—a horrendous roar that echoed and bounced down the metal canyon of buildings.

Turning to look, Bumblebee saw the terrifying Grimlock stalking down the street, moving past Caesar's Palace in his Tyrannosaurus Rex form. Throwing his head back, Grimlock once more raked the night with his awesome challenge.

A challenge to anyone stupid enough to defy him.

"Decepticons no can win this fight," he growled in

his guttural dialect. "I now here to finish what other Autobots not able to." Behind Grimlock, a small army of helicopters swooped through the pulsing lights, while several tanks attempted to make their way down the packed street without crushing cars.

Grimlock's words angered Bumblebee—after all, he and Prowl hadn't done too badly. But Bumblebee wasn't about to stand up to the leader of the Dinobots, especially after Grimlock had all but renounced his ties to the other Autobots and Optimus Prime. Even in the flashing lights, Bumblebee could see the gleaming scar where Grimlock had torn off his own Autobot symbol. He and Prowl had stayed with Grimlock only because of their inability to find Optimus themselves, and because of Grimlock's avowed hatred of the Decepticons.

That Grimlock could take both of them out without overtaxing a single servomotor had nothing to do with it. Where the Decepticons were concerned, you took allies where you found them.

"Of all the Autobots, I thought for sure that you would not care about these biological parasites," Soundwave mocked Grimlock as he strode out of the darkness near the Luxor casino. "Does the mighty Grimlock have a weakness after all?"

"Grimlock not Autobot!" Grimlock growled back, his anger apparent in his flashing eyes. His mechanical jaws gnashed the air, as though he could already feel them crushing the last electronic impulses from Soundwave's body. "Grimlock care about destroying Decepticons." With that loud proclamation, he moved forward, his pace slow but inexorable.

The wounded Thundercracker exploded up out of the rubble in front of Caesar's Palace. Sailing through the air, he came down behind Grimlock and hammered into his back with both fists.

Grimlock shrugged off the assault as though it had not occurred. He spun around, surprisingly fast for his size, and knocked Thundercracker off his feet with a quick swipe of his tail. With another roar that shook the night, Grimlock raised a mighty clawed foot and smashed it down upon Thundercracker's chest, causing the protective plating to buckle. Though Thundercracker attempted to retreat, Grimlock was unmerciful and drove his foot into the downed Decepticons chest three more times until he lay still, his sensors obviously scrambled for the time being.

With a roar of victory, Grimlock dismissed his fallen enemy and turned back to continue his forward march toward Soundwave.

Soundwave immediately raised both arms, his hands transforming into large radar dishes. Bumblebee threw himself backwards as the visible wall of sound avalanched down the street. Even Grimlock grunted as the shockwave slammed into him, but his clawed feet simply dug into the pavement, and he continued to move forward as though the energy being unleashed was merely a light gale.

The helicopters, on the other hand, were not faring so well. Several were swatted from the sky, with the rest having to pull back or risk crashing themselves.

With a start, Bumblee realized that for such a confrontation, it was highly unlikely that Soundwave had only brought along Thundercracker. What other Decepticons were waiting in the wings for the right moment to pounce on Grimlock? Though he felt almost powerless next to Grimlock's awesome might, he knew that even the monstrous leader of the Dinobots could be taken down if enough Decepticons surprised him.

In a blur of motion, Bumblebee transformed into car mode and shot down the street, heading north, away from the combat zone. Hitting Flamingo Road, he turned left and accelerated, moving between vehicles quicker and with more agility than any human driver could hope to mimic. He shot over the freeway, knowing it was unlikely that any Decepticon would travel that route. At Valley View, he turned left again and began running parallel to Las Vegas Boulevard, his sensors searching the night for any unusual readings.

The sounds of battle continued, with bright flashes that even eclipsed the normal brilliance of the city. The angry roar of Grimlock added a sonic counterpoint, and additional gunfire announced that at least some of his human army had managed to enter the combat.

Continuing to weave in and out of traffic, Bumblebee flew down the road, then turned left onto Tropicana, moving perpendicular to the combat. Shooting past close to the battle, he saw Soundwave and Grimlock engaged in hand-to-hand combat. Though Grimlock was far superior in strength, Soundwave's speed made up the difference as the twin giants pummeled each other.

Bumblebee turned left again, and was just beginning to think that perhaps Soundwave had been foolhardy enough to come on his own, when a jet rocketed past him in the direction of the melee. At the same time, his sensors picked up another robot moving toward the battle from the other direction.

For a moment, Bumblebee was stunned when he

realized that the one of the Decepticons' sneakiest operators was here. Had Skywarp joined Starscream now as well? The powerful Decepticon had always been firmly in Megatron's control, and his being here could only mean additional trouble. Not to mention that fact that Skywarp's teleportation abilities would certainly catch Grimlock by surprise.

"Grimlock! Skywarp is heading toward your position!" he yelled into his broadcast. He pushed his speed up over a hundred miles an hour—a yellow blur that passed cars as though they were mired in tar.

"Grimlock, you oversized lizard, answer me!" Bumblebee knew that such a wisecrack might get him a tail lashing, but he had to break through the Dinobot's battle-crazed fury. If Skywarp got off a good shot when Grimlock was not looking...Bumblebee didn't want to think about it.

He skidded around the corner to follow Skywarp, tires squealing. In this direction, Skywarp was heading toward Las Vegas Boulevard, and would be almost right on top of Grimlock and Soundwave. Desperate for any plan, Bumblebee shot forward at maximum acceleration. What could he do against a Decepticon as powerful as Skywarp? Up ahead, Skywarp slowed in midair, and spun to the left. Realizing that Skywarp was going to hit Grimlock from behind with everything he had, Bumblebee grew almost frantic. Then, stopped at the intersection ahead of him, he saw a car-hauling semi-truck, empty, with its back ramp in the lowered position. Without a thought for himself, Bumblebee raced forward and launched skyward from the top of the ramp.

Bumblebee knew that with Optimus Prime missing,

only Grimlock could hope to stop Starscream and his Decepticons from completely conquering Las Vegas, then the rest of the world. He had to do whatever it took.

"Behind you, Grimlock!" he roared in a voice uncharacteristically loud. His timing was perfect. He passed between the unsuspecting Dinobot and Skywarp just as the Decepticon unleashed his powerful missile launchers. The blast struck Bumblebee squarely in the chest, his circuits screaming, even as he transformed in midair. He fell to the ground, landing in a giant fountain, barely able to move or even think. He could feel his systems trying to compensate.

Grimlock roared his anger at Skywarp's sneak attack, swung his might tail in one direction and then, using all of his awesome strength, swung it back around and slammed it into Skywarp. The force of the blow created a thunderclap that split the night air, and Skywarp was sent flying through the air for several miles almost due north.

Everything seemed to be in slow motion, and Bumblebee felt like his systems were running at less than quarter speed. He thought he was forgetting something. Something important. Grimlock turned his attention back to Soundwave, who had retreated by several long strides and looked extraordinarily happy with himself.

"Get ready, Grimlock," the Decepticon shouted. "Today, you die!"

The ground shook as, from behind one of the casinos, the titanic form of Devastator appeared.

Bumblebee felt himself being lifted out of the fountain, and turned his head. It was Prowl.

"Come on, Bumblebee," he said. "This is no time for a bath. We've got to get out of here."

"But Grimlock," Bumblebee mumbled. "He's going to need help."

"So are we, if we try to fight Devastator." Even as the words left Prowl's mouth, Grimlock engaged the giant form of this new opponent. Devastator slammed a mighty fist into his jaw, forcing the Dinobot backwards. The sound of splitting metal could be heard for miles.

"Let's *go*," Prowl said. "We've got to get back to Optimus and Jazz."

"Optimus?" Bumblebee said, his confused circuits still working on getting his systems back in order.

"You didn't see him?" Prowl said, shoving Bumblebee to his feet. "He's back, along with Jazz and a whole bunch of humans and aliens. We're going to need his help."

Bumblebee shook his head. It seemed like things were happening too fast for him to keep up. "All right," he said, still not wanting to abandon Grimlock. "But what about Grimlock?"

Prowl studied the two combatants, who were smashing through buildings and destroying entire city blocks with their fighting. It was clear who had the upper hand: Devastator. And in the meantime, Grimlock's human allies were being driven backward by Soundwave.

"I don't think there's much we can do for him," Prowl said. "It's time to go."

They both transformed, though Bumblebee knew he needed serious repairs, and together they headed off in the direction of downtown, where Optimus and Jazz were just a short time ago.

Behind them, Soundwave's voice called out, "Decepticons! Attack!"

Prowl and Bumblebee knew that the real battle was just getting started and they both put everything they had available into one goal: escape.

FOUR

When the teeming mass of life-forms surged through the gate, detective Paul Chateris didn't know for certain what awaited them on the other side. He did know that he'd best hit the ground running—there was sure to be chaos with all these people, aliens and machines trying to escape the Keepers. As he stepped through, he reached out and grabbed Melony's hand, shouting in her ear to be heard over the noise, "No matter what happens, don't let go of me!"

A wrenching pain stabbed at him for a split second as they passed through the shimmering energy field, and then they were on the other side. Paul immediately recognized the location: Las Vegas. A neon sign, hanging by its wires but still glowing, announced that he was near the Seven Wonders and More Casino. And as he suspected, things were quite a mess.

Aliens, unable to adapt to the environment, were scattered like children's toys all over the landscape. Rescue workers struggled to get through the debris, and in the distance, Decepticons appeared to be waging war on…each other. People were shoving to get by him, and Melony was nearly yanked from his grasp.

He pulled her forward at a jog, knowing that to run could mean missing something that might just get them killed. At they crossed the street, a jagged piece of metal—what appeared to be the back quarter-panel of some car—flew over their heads to embed itself in a wall. Paul spotted an alley that looked like promising shelter and headed for it. Once there, he let go of Melony's hand and took up a position where he could observe the raging scene across the street.

"Now what?" she asked. Her face was pale and drawn, but in truth she looked more angry than frightened. She was an olive-skinned woman, beautiful even now, with long black hair that ran in straight, shining lines down her back.

Paul remembered what the Keepers had shown him. Melony's sister dying during a battle between the Autobots and the Decepticons, her hate and guilt. The woman was not stable, but she was obviously torn between fear and hate. He couldn't just leave her here—though he was sorely tempted. He needed to report in to his boss. "I'm not sure," he said. "But going out there is a seriously bad idea."

As he watched, Megatron and Starscream burst out of a wall, intertwined and hurling curses at each other, and streaked into the sky on Starscream's jets. Megatron did not look like he was faring well. The other Decepticons followed on the ground. The battle appeared to be moving away from them—for now.

"Good enough for me," Paul said. "It's time for us to move on while we can. Is there somewhere I can take you?"

Melony shook her head. "Not really. I don't know anyone here."

Paul nodded. "I figured as much. Let's see if we can

find the nearest police station. At worst, we should be able to get some more information about what's going on."

They ducked back out of the alley cautiously, but the worst of the fighting seemed to have stopped. Now, Optimus Prime and Jazz were working feverishly to try and save as many of the aliens as possible. The Keepers appeared to be meditating or something, huddled together like flesh-machines out of some Van Gogh nightmare.

Spotting a uniformed officer nearby, Paul trotted across the street, Melony close behind. "Hey!" Paul said, as they approached.

The cop spun around so fast, Paul thought for a moment he was going to complete a full circle. He held up his hands, "Whoa! Just a civilian," he said. "Stay calm."

The cop sighed audibly. He was young, probably no more than thirty. "Sorry about that," he said. "It's a jumpy sort of day." He looked at the street filled with wreckage. "What can I do for you?"

"Just need directions to the nearest station," Paul said, in his most charming manner. He was a good-looking man, ruggedly handsome with dark features—a fact he'd often used to set others, even men, at ease. "I could use some information."

The officer looked at him suspiciously. "Are you a reporter?"

Paul shook his head and laughed. "Not hardly," he said. He pulled out his badge. "I'm a plainclothes, out of New York." He pointed across the street. "I was one of those taken."

The good thing about being a cop, Paul had often noticed, was that you had brothers and sisters in every city and small town in America. "No kidding?" he said. "They'll want to talk with you anyway."

Paul smiled. "I sort of figured they might. But right now, I could use information, directions, and maybe a cell phone."

"Not a problem," the officer said. "Say, my name's Kelly. John Kelly." He stuck out his hand.

Paul shook it, never suspecting a thing. So when the jolt of electricity went through him, he never said a word. Just heard Melony shouting his name as he went down into the darkness.

"Paul, wake up!"

In the darkness of his mind, Paul stirred. Someone was calling him.

"Come on, Paul. You've got to get up!"

Up, he thought. *I need to get up.I don't want to get up. I hurt.*

He rolled over on his side and groaned. Every muscle in his body protested the movement. *Nope, definetely not getting up.*

"Paul, you need to wake up. They're coming." It was Melony's voice. The one filled with equal parts hate and fear.

Who's coming? Paul opened his eyes. "Who?" he asked.

"The Decepticons," she said. "Come on. You need to get moving."

Paul struggled into a sitting position, trying to remember. His mind and body felt like jelly and it was hard to concentrate. "What happened?" he asked.

"That cop you were talking to zapped you with some kind of tazer built into his arm. That's why your muscles ache and you're having a hard time focusing. It will pass."

Now Paul remembered. He felt a surge of annoyance that he'd been taken in by one of his own. He looked around the small room. At least he wasn't in a cell. It was about fifteen by ten, with aqua-green walls. A large table dominated the center of the space, its slate gray top scarred by cigarette burns. There were three folding chairs around the table. The cot he was sitting on didn't belong here. This was an interrogation room.

He looked at Melony. "How long?"

"I'm not sure," she said. "My watch stopped working when we came through the gate. Maybe a couple of hours."

Paul nodded. "I've never heard of a tazer knocking someone out for two hours, let alone being embedded in someone's arm like that."

"Me, either."

Voices were raised outside the door, which rattled with a key and then opened. A tall, beefy man with gray hair and a nose that looked like it had been broken multiple times stepped into the room. He shut the door behind him. Paul heard it being locked from the outside.

The man tossed Paul's wallet on the table, then stepped over and offered a hand to Paul. "I'm Lomax," he said. "Chief of Vegas PD."

Paul looked carefully at the outstretched hand. "The last time I shook hands with a Vegas cop, I took a hell of a jolt," he said. "Not sure I care to repeat the experience."

Lomax pulled his hand back. "I know. Sorry about that. It's SOP. Since Starscream took over, we've had a few problems with spies and freelancers coming in here to save the day." His voice took on a sarcastic tone with the last few words. He sighed. "Whenever a strange cop shows up now, we zap 'em and bring 'em in for questioning until we're sure they're here for legit reasons." He offered the hand again. "No shock this time. I promise."

Paul took the offered hand, and Lomax pulled him to his feet. "Those new tazers the Decepticons gave us pack a hell of a wallop, but the effects will pass soon enough." He gestured to the table. "Have a seat," he said. Lomax had a voice that was deep and smooth. Paul thought he recognized the type already: a politician in cop clothes.

He and Melony both took chairs on the other side of the table. Paul picked up his wallet and thumbed through it. Everything was still there.

"I'm a little confused," Paul said. "Starscream has taken over Las Vegas?"

Lomax chuckled. "Kelly said you told him you were one of the ones taken by the Keepers. This must seem pretty damned odd."

Paul nodded. "Last I checked, Megatron was the leader of the Decepticons. And I can't honestly imagine that he'd just hand the reins over to Starscream."

"Megatron was gone and, as far as anyone knew, maybe for good. Starscream leads the Decepticons now."

For some reason, the man seemed immensely pleased by this, though Paul couldn't imagine why. "Interesting," he said. "But now that Megatron is back—"

"He and Starscream reached quite an understanding out there in the desert," Lomax said, grinning broadly.

"Megatron has relinquished the leadership of the Decepticons."

Paul sat back in his chair, stunned. He remembered Starscream all too well.

"So the Decepticons completely control Las Vegas?" Melony asked.

"Pretty much," Lomax said. "Though these 'Keepers' have added a wrinkle we didn't quite expect."

"Hold on a minute," Paul said. "Since when do the cops work for the Decepticons?"

Lomax chuckled. "Since they raised our pay by a hundred and fifty percent, armed us decently, and helped to ensure that the bad guys—street thugs, drug dealers and killers—get caught and go to jail."

Paul nodded, inwardly seething. The Decepticons were *evil*, no matter what it looked like. "Makes sense," he said. "I could use a pay raise myself."

"I bet," Lomax said. "I checked your bonafides, of course. Your chief thought you were probably dead."

"I'm tougher than I look," Paul said.

"Excuse me?" Melony said. "I think it's wonderful that you two boys in blue can clap each other on the back with a hail-fellow-well-met attitude. I really do. But I haven't done anything wrong. I've been captured by aliens, taken to some other world where they used us as informational guinea pigs, and then sent back to find that the Decepticons have taken over Las Vegas. I just want to go home now. Is that all right?"

Lomax nodded. "I understand how you feel, Miss. I really do. But orders *are* orders. And I've been ordered to hold both of you for questioning by Starscream himself. He has lots of things he wants to know about these so-called Keepers...before he crushes them like bugs."

Paul and Melony couldn't help themselves. They both burst out laughing. Deep, gut-wrenching laughs that came from their toes.

Lomax first looked puzzled, then annoyed. "What the hell's so funny?" he demanded, glaring at the two of them while they laughed like fools.

"Oh, God," Paul said, gasping and trying to catch his breath. "You wouldn't know, would you? None of you would." If the situation weren't so desperate, Paul realized, the fact that the joke was on Starscream would be *really* funny.

"What…" Lomax almost yelled.

"These Keepers," Paul said, finally gaining control of himself. "They aren't little green men come to share technology. Their powers make the Transformers look like wind-up toys. These creatures are practically *gods*," he said.

Melony nodded. "They'll destroy everything."

"They're more powerful than the Transformers?" Lomax gasped.

Paul shook his head. "The comparison doesn't even apply." He stared at Lomax, his eyes cold and hard. "If they want, this whole planet will be nothing more than a zoo for their amusement."

CHAPTER

FIVE

His name was Allister Greaves. At seventy-five, he looked like a man in his mid-fifties. His hair was a dark, wavy black highlighted by white, swept back from his forehead, full and luxurious. Standing almost six-four, with eyes that ranged from the ice-blue of an arctic lake to the slate gray of mountain storms, he was an imposing figure. Allister believed in dressing the part, so his clothes were tailored suits, and his cane, which he carried habitually, was a single, long stick of some wood that was almost black. The cane top, a silver wolf's head, was his personal symbol—he knew it was better to be a predator than prey.

And he was the man behind the Followers.

To someone observing him, seated at a long table in his ornate dining room, with the light of a crystal chandelier shining down, he could have simply been a rich man having a solitary meal. He was, in fact, eating a meal: baked game hen with a mustard and dill glaze, sautéed carrots with brown sugar, au gratin potatoes with leeks, and a small, hearts of romaine salad with blue-cheese dressing. Much like his clothing, Allister believed in eating with decorum, so he took measured bites, chewing carefully, blotting his lips from time to time with a white linen napkin, sipping on a glass of Chardonnay to cleanse his palate. The same someone observing him might suspect he was deep in thought, which he was. But his thoughts stemmed from the information being fed into his left ear by a tiny device that he had invented himself.

Allister Greaves was nothing if not inventive.

At present, the information he was receiving in his was a garbled recording of a phone call placed by one of his Followers in Los Angeles. It went to an unassigned number, was recorded and then transferred to yet another number, and still another number. The transfer of data was almost instant. With the aid of a device concealed within his suit coat, Allister could listen to any number of recorded calls, tune into several news networks, and even pick up various free frequency broadcasts. He had played this particular call several times over.

"This is Stuckey in north L.A. I don't know what's happening. Everyone here saw the broadcast of the Transformers return along with the aliens. A short time after, a wall of...Jesus...a wall of blackness appeared to the south. Distant at first, but moving closer. It wasn't clouds. I know it's not clouds. But it's coming closer and you can't see behind it. It's like something out of a movie, but there's no sound. Can you hear me? There's no sound...."

There was a long pause on the recording and Allister could hear the man's heavy breathing. The call log indicated that he made the call on his cell phone, so he must have been watching whatever it was come closer.

"I don't know what to do. I don't think running will help. If this has something to do with the Transformers' return, some new manifestation of their powers, then I must...Jesus, I'm scared...I must see what's in the cloud. It's moving up the street. Silent and black. Nothing is inside it, nothing I can see behind it. I'm going to go now. It's coming. I'll call again if I can."

The line went dead.

Allister shook his head. The world was about to change again. He pushed a button on the tabletop and a small videophone rose up. He dialed a number from memory. The call didn't go through. He selected a different number. And again. And again. All calls placed to Los Angeles didn't go through.

He selected a different number. The voice on the other end of the line answered, darkly feminine. "Yes? Hello?"

Allister smiled. She was using a French accent this time. The next time he called, it would be Swedish or Russian. She was quite charming that way. "Elisa," he said, his voice was cultured and mellow. "It's Allister."

"*Monsieur* Greaves," she said. "What a pleasant surprise. Though I can say I *was* expecting your call."

"I'm certain you were, my dear. Can you tell me anything about the situation in Los Angeles?"

She sighed into the receiver. "Very little, I'm afraid," she said. "A squadron of jet fighters was dispatched to investigate a black cloud that has completely encircled the city. They flew in, but went out of radio contact immediately. Best estimates say they ran out of fuel about forty-five minutes ago."

"They're gone then," Allister said. It was not a question.

"Without a doubt," she answered.

"Anything else?" he asked.

"Yes," she said. "There's a cabinet meeting in an hour or so to discuss these new aliens...the Keepers. Do you want the transcript?"

"Of course," Allister said. "Anything you've got."

"I'll send it later today," she promised.

"You're wonderful, Elisa. What would I do without you?" Not for the first time, it crossed Allister's mind to bring this woman to work for him on a full-time basis, but he immediately dismissed the thought. She was far too valuable where she was.

"Hire someone else?" she asked playfully.

"You are not so easily replaced," he said, meaning it. "I will contact you later."

"*Bonjour, mon amour*," she said.

Allister broke the connection and stared thoughtfully at the phone for several minutes. For now, it was safe to assume that Los Angeles—such as it was after an off-shore nuclear blast had reduced it to a near wasteland—was no more. The Keepers had, at least, picked a target that wasn't a completely tragic loss. That said, he had over a dozen operatives in the area—most likely they were dead.

He also wondered what was keeping two of his operatives in Las Vegas from calling in. One had been in regular contact until today's events; the other, Allister had seen come through the gate with the Transformers and the aliens. Why hadn't Paul gotten in touch yet?

He needed information before he could move.

The Transformers represented power—power that he wanted, and wanted to understand. The Keepers, on the other hand, obviously represented a unique power, too. Perhaps an even stronger one than the

Transformers themselves. Allister wasn't certain if this was a good thing or not. It was possible that they represented too *much* power, and were a threat to his plans. It was equally possible that they could help him achieve his plans on a scale he'd never before dreamed possible.

Allister was a wolf. He would be patient, though it sorely vexed him. Sooner or later, it would become clear which of the paths he should take: capture and explore (and exploit) the Transformers; capture and explore (and exploit) the Keepers; both or none of the above.

He looked at the phone again, adjusted the device in his pocket and checked for forwarded messages. There were none. People were in shock. And most of the Followers, he suspected, were dismayed to find out that those beings they had considered almost god-like had competition in the universe for supremacy.

Allister looked at his watch. If Paul or his other chief operative in Las Vegas didn't contact him within the next two or three hours, he'd try to reach them directly. He *needed* to know what was happening in Las Vegas. And he needed it now.

He pushed a button, and the phone retracted back into the table. He then rang a small bell that would let his servants know that they could come and clear away the lunch dishes.

As he walked back toward his study, he thought again about the call from the Los Angeles operative. *"It's coming....there's no sound."*

What *was* happening out there?

After hanging up his phone, Stuckey purposefully walked into the middle of the deserted street. Those who were going to try and flee the rapidly advancing cloud of darkness had long since run for their lives. *He would not.*

It was only a few blocks away, a solid wall of pitch darkness. As it moved closer, he realized that he could see...reflections on it, as though it were made of polished jet or onyx. But it moved fluidly, and whatever it swallowed up didn't cause even the slightest stir on its surface.

He breathed deeply. *I'm scared witless*, he thought. *But this could be the work of the Transformers...or those other creatures.* Stuckey began walking slowly toward it.

The silence in the street was oppressive, and for the first time, he noticed that his whole body was covered in a thin film of sweat, though the air was almost cold. In fact, he realized, it *was* cold. Not the usual temperature for irradiated L.A. at all.

The wall of whatever it was moved closer. Stuckey could see his own reflection now. *Why doesn't it make any noise?* He stared at it thoughtfully as he walked. It should make *some* kind of noise, he thought, even the crunch of pavement passing beneath it.

He was perhaps ten or fifteen feet away when he stopped. Fear made him tremble, and he could feel the temperature dropping rapidly, as if the thing were a solid wall of ice. Some sort of titanic glacier of darkness.

Part of him wanted to run—run like hell—but he had to stay. He had to find out what was inside it, on the other side of it.

He forced himself to take a step forward, then another. His mind raced and gibbered like an insane monkey. *Run, you fool!*

And that's when he felt it. It was pulling him closer. Like a vacuum. But there was no sound of rushing air, and the pull was almost gentle—an insistent lover telling him to come back to bed and go to sleep.

That's when he tried to run and found that for all its gentleness, the pull wouldn't let him escape. He struggled and thrashed, finally falling to the pavement in a heap.

As the advancing wall overtook him, he felt his legs go completely numb in an instant. He tried to scream, but the air was now so cold that his breath came out as nothing more than a ragged wheeze. It climbed over his body, a slow, steady inch at a time, freezing him as it went.

In the final seconds before it closed over his head, Stuckey realized that he could hear something after all: his blood cells, freezing and popping, deep inside his heart.

Then he heard nothing at all.

CHAPTER

SIX

For a long second, Optimus Prime stared down the street, trying to make sense of the scene before him. Bumblebee, his armor scorched and damaged, was running full-tilt alongside Prowl. They were bashing through cars, building debris and anything else that stood in their way. Behind them, a full force of Decepticons were giving chase. Optimus adjusted his sensors. In the distance, he could hear Grimlock roaring and fighting Devastator, as well as the sound of human combat units.

"Everybody get down!" Optimus yelled. Aliens and humans alike took one look at the oncoming forces and scattered like chickens before wolves. *I don't blame them a bit*, Optimus thought. Everyone ran except Spike and Franklin, who knelt down beside an abandoned ambulance.

"Bumblebee, Prowl! To me!" Optimus brought up his laser rifle, sighting in on the nearest opponent: a black menace in the shape of a hawk who was called Buzzsaw. He fired, the bolt arcing through the night air to slam into Buzzsaw's wing. The metallic hawk veered off, but not before launching a volley of missiles from his own guns. The missiles slammed into the concrete, blowing huge chunks from the ground.

"Optimus," Prowl called, "he's running on empty!" He turned and spun, bringing his own weapon up to provide cover for the ailing Bumblebee.

Leaping forward, Optimus ran to get between the little yellow robot and his pursuers. On his left, Jazz sent up a barrage of fire. Several of the Decepticons took glancing hits as they dove for cover. Apparently intent on their prey, they hadn't seen the waiting Autobots.

"Optimus," Jazz yelled, trying to be heard over the noise, "did you see that?"

Reaching the ailing Bumblebee, Optimus turned to glance down the street. Prowl was firing as fast as he could, backing up all the while, while Jazz also kept up a barrage of steady fire. Peering past the smoke, Optimus saw a Decepticon unfamiliar to him. Massively built, and easily as large as Devastator, Prime felt a sliver of worry pierce him.

If there were Decepticons on the planet he didn't know about, that could mean a *huge* problem, Optimus thought. And he'd never seen this particular Decepticon. Black and gold heavy armor, with weapons ranging from mortars to slag knew what else...*I wonder where he's been hiding all this time.*

"Jazz, Prowl," he ordered, "try to hold them off for a few minutes."

"You got it!" Jazz yelled, resuming his barrage of fire. Prowl, looking a little battleworn himself, finally managed to get side-by-side with Jazz. The various Decepticons slipped around the backside of the building, and Prime knew he only had a couple of minutes at the most. He turned his attention to Bumblebee.

"How you doing, soldier?" he asked.

"Prime," Bumblebee said, "I stopped him! I kept Skywarp from killing Grimlock!"

Prime nodded. "You did good," he said. He began assessing the damage the young Autobot had sustained. It was bad enough to require immediate repair.

Bumblebee's voice stuttered a bit, then he added, "We had to leave him, Optimus. I'm sorry."

"Nothing to be sorry for," Prime said. "You did what you could." He cocked his head to one side. "It sounds like he's still in the fight."

Bumblebee shook his head. "Not for long," he muttered.

"Why?" Prime asked, beginning to make lightning-fast repairs that should help hold Bumblebee together long enough to get him back to headquarters.

"He's trying to fight Skywarp, Soundwave and Devastator all at once."

"That's going to go tough on him, all right," Prime said. He finished a final adjustment. "That's about all I can do from here," he said. "Can you transform back into car mode?"

Bumblebee staggered to his feet. As he transformed, Prime could hear metal crunching against metal. It wasn't a good sound at all, but somehow Bumblebee made it into vehicle mode. "Good deal," Prime said. "Let's get out of here." He looked to his fellow warriors. "Jazz, Prowl, it's time to go!"

Both stopped firing long enough to risk a glance at their leader. In the street, the unknown Decepticon began a slow, methodical advance. *That Decepticon is truly mighty*, Prime thought.

"Couldn't be a better time," Jazz said.

"We're going to need some help to defeat this many Decepticons," Prowl said. He took a long, hard look at the advancing enemy. "A *lot* of help."

"I agree," Prime said. "Transform into vehicle mode. Jazz, you take Spike and Franklin with you."

The two robots transformed quickly, and Jazz's doors opened.

"Spike," Franklin said. "I'll catch up to you later. I can find you if I need to."

"You're not leaving?" Prime asked, incredulous. "Have your enhancements made you mad?"

Franklin laughed. "I don't believe so," he said. "But if you're going to escape, that thing needs something else to shoot at. I *might* be fast enough to elude it."

"Franklin!" Spike said. "Don't be stupid."

Glancing at Decepticon, who was even now beginning to target their area, Franklin snapped, "I'm not stupid. Far from it. Now get out of here!" He turned and ran with amazing speed *toward* the oncoming titan.

Prime shook his head. "Let's not allow his sacrifice to be for nothing. Autobots, roll out!"

He transformed, then led the others away at top speed. Behind them, he saw a flash as the Decepticon fired multiple mortar rounds, their massive firepower evidenced by the flare of red flames as they slammed into the ground where the Autobots had been only seconds before.

"Keep moving," Prime commanded. He tried to see if he could sense Franklin, wondering again about the agent's stability, but the man was gone…and the Decepticon—whatever he was—was actually turning around! What in the world was going on back there?

And why had the unknown Decepticon waited so long to attack, as though he was…restrained in some fashion.

As they sped away into the deepening night, Optimus figured that it wouldn't be all that long before they found out.

Late that night, safely ensconced in the Autobot headquarters, Prime sat and listened as Spike filled him in on what had happened since Prime, Jazz and Bluestreak had been taken by the Keepers.

"So," Prime said, "Starscream now commands the Decepticons. That's not something I'm sure I care for. Megatron's hate and cynicism cause him to have a fairly direct approach—even when he thinks he's being sneaky. Starscream, on the other hand, is much more devious and subtle."

"You've got that right," Spike said. "Why do you suppose he chose to take over Las Vegas? Why not New York or Chicago or even Washington, D.C.?"

"I don't know, Spike," Prime said. "But I'm sure there *is* a reason. Starscream wouldn't pick the city at random."

"But does he even *control* it?" Spike wondered. "With all the battles there, and now the Keepers, I think he's probably got his hands full."

Prime nodded, thinking of the Keepers' edict. News reports, sketchy as they were, out of the area around Los Angeles, weren't good. The Keepers had not been joking: Los Angeles appeared to be completely obliterated. Where it once stood, or what was left of it after the nuclear blast, was a wall of blackness. Everything sent in disappeared, and didn't come out.

"It's only a matter of time—three days, they

said—until the Keepers move to solidify their hold on this world. Before then, we must act to stop them," Prime said.

"I still can't believe it about Bluestreak," Spike said. "He…"

"I know," Prime said. "But we cannot allow ourselves the luxury of mourning his loss. He was a good friend, and a good fighter—but he is no more, anymore than Sentinal Prime is. We must focus our attention on the Keepers."

Spike nodded. "How powerful are they really?" he asked.

Prime looked at the young human who had been so close to them. He thought about his family and his still unexplained association with Franklin—who was, in Prime's estimation, much more than he appeared. "They are powerful enough to destroy this world and make it their own playground," he said.

"So what do we do?" Spike asked.

"*We* do nothing," Prime said. "You have risked enough for us by bringing us back. The man you associate with, Franklin, is not to be trusted. My instinct tells me this." Prime shook his head, thinking of all the lives already lost in fruitless battles. "You should go home to your family."

"No can do, Optimus," Spike said. "They're in custody, being held pending my cooperation with Franklin's agency. And in order for him to get what he wants, we're going to have to stop the Keepers."

"We can't just stop them, Spike," Prime said. "They must be utterly annihilated."

Prime had never heard his own voice grow so cold. Yet he knew it had to be done. If humanity was to have any chance of survival at all, the Keepers had to be destroyed.

"And how can we do that?" Spike asked. "If they were powerful enough to capture you and Megatron and force you to do all those things…you said it took the power of the Matrix to bend them to your will at all! And they may be even more powerful here."

"I am aware of that, Spike," Optimus said. "We have little choice. The Decepticons and the Autobots must set aside their differences for now and form an alliance."

"WHAT…" Spike said. "But Optimus, that's—"

Prime held up a hand for silence. His circuits and servomotors were in need of repair from his time on the Keepers' world. "Insane," he said. "Yes, I know." He shook his head again, thinking not only of how things had changed so quickly here on Earth in their absence, but his promised favor to Megatron back on the Keepers' world. How long before Megatron, now deposed as the leader of the Decepticons, would decide to cash in? "Spike, it's the only choice we have. Unless the Decepticons and the Autobots team up, the Keepers will win. They will destroy us all."

Sitting there with his mouth open, Spike looked like he'd been hit in the head with a hammer.

"Spike, you must trust me in this," Optimus said. "The Keepers evil knows no bounds. They *are* more powerful than we are."

"How much more?" Spike asked, his voice sounding strangely small and quiet.

"Vastly, I'm afraid," Optimus said. "We are nothing more than children's toys to them."

The silence in the room was very loud after that,

and the two old friends said nothing for quite some time.

CHAPTER

SEVEN

The front lawn of the MGM Grand had been cleared of debris from the recent fighting, and for now, the only noises were from the Decepticon spectators waiting and watching to see Megatron officially surrender command to Starscream. Inwardly, Megatron was seething. It took every ounce of his self-control not to rush headlong across the lush green sward and rip Starscream limb from limb.

Outwardly, he remained calm. It wouldn't do to let Starscream know of his plans, but he'd continually been surprised by the depth of Starscream's plans...as he was now.

On one end of the area, a makeshift throne had been erected. Behind it, the hulking Devastator and a powerful Decepticon Megatron himself had found and put on ice for the future flanked the new Decepticon leader. He was Omega Sentinel—sent to Earth long ago to search for Omega Sentinel. As strong as Devastator, but coldly logical like the missing Shockwave, with amazingly strong armor and weapons, Omega Sentinel had been meant as a surprise for the Autobots...but now it seemed that Starscream had found him and converted his loyalty to himself. It was one more thing to hate Starscream for—wasting a weapon as important as Omega Sentinel on his own vanity.

Several others stood nearby, talking with their new "lord." Megatron stood next to Soundwave, waiting for Starscream to call him forward. *He'll play it for everything it's worth*, Megatron thought.

"You don't have to do this," Soundwave hissed. "If you fight him, a number of the others will come over to you."

Megatron nodded. "I am aware of that, Soundwave. Your loyalty is noted and will be remembered. But for now Starscream has the advantage. He has those two," he said, pointing to the titanic forms behind the throne.

"But, Megatron...

Megatron held up a hand and Soundwave immediately fell silent. "No, Soundwave. And now is not the time. Starscream in his madness may not realize it, but the Keepers are far more important an enemy than I am, or even the Autobots."

"They are aliens," Soundwave acknowledged, "but we've dealt with aliens before."

"Not like these," Megatron said. "They are far more dangerous than any other species we've ever encountered." He paused, thinking of the news that Los Angeles was gone, and the Keepers' three-day time limit to surrender. "And they must be stopped."

Soundwave was about to reply, when Starscream's arrogant, high-pitched voice sounded across the lawn, silencing the other Decepticons. "Megatron! Step forward."

Megatron strode across the lawn. He could still feel the strain on his servomotors and circuits from his battles on the Keepers' world as well as from his fight with Starscream. Hopefully, there would be someone tonight who could begin the process of helping him repair the damage. As he passed among the Decepticons he had led for such a long time, Megatron spared them not a glance. If they looked at him, saw his face, they might well read that he had no intention whatsoever of allowing Starscream to keep command of the Decepticons.

He was simply smart enough to know when to play along. Much like he had with the Keepers.

He reached the area directly before the throne. Again, the temptation to throttle the mad traitor was almost more than he could bear. But…there were the Keepers to deal with first. Then, and only then, would he allow himself the luxury of ripping Starscream to pieces and casting his broken remains into a lava pit.

Megatron looked at Starscream, who had long craved the leadership of the Decepticons. Perhaps a taste of the real thing would give him some pause….

"Megatron," Starscream said, "the time has come at last. It will be as it should have been from the beginning—*I* will lead the Decepticons, and *you* will follow."

"I said I would agree to hand over leadership of the Decepticons to you, Starscream. I did *not* say I would follow."

"*What*?" Starscream bellowed. "You would dare to play false with me?"

"Not false!" Megatron said. "I will willingly surrender my role as leader, but I will *not* follow you, Starscream. You are a traitor, and worse—you would rather waste precious time trying to make me surrender to you in public when there are much bigger problems to be dealt with. You have already proven that you would rather *play* at being a leader than actually being one."

The other Decepticons gathered began to talk amongst themselves.

"What do you mean by this?" Starscream asked.

"I mean the Keepers," Megatron said. "They are powerful beyond anything we've ever previously encountered. And unless we move to stop them, they will destroy us all."

"I will contend with the Keepers in good time," Starscream sneered. "They are no real threat to me...any more than you are."

"I assumed you would believe that," Megatron said. He turned to the assembled Decepticons. "I hereby relinquish my role as the leader of the Decepticons to Starscream. If one of you should feel that you are better suited to the task than he is, by all means, feel free to try and take it from him. Further, I hereby declare that I am no longer one of you." He ripped his Decepticon badge off in one smooth stroke. "Until such time as the Keepers are dealt with, I won't be associated with any leader who denies their powers. To do so is a sure sign of madness."

He turned back to Starscream and tossed the metallic badge into his lap. "There," he said, "I've surrendered the leadership to you—much good it will do you."

"*You* must submit to me!" Starscream screeched.

"I will not!" Megatron said. "You rule the Decepticons now, Starscream, but I am no longer a Decepticon." He turned and began the walk back across the lawn of the casino, his plans coalescing in his mind.

"You *must* kneel before me!" Starscream howled behind his back. He ignored him.

As he passed the other Decepticons, he nodded to several. They immediately walked to the front of the throne.

Soundwave was the first to reach the raving Starscream. "He has the right to do this, Starscream, and you know it. He can leave and you cannot prevent him from doing so. The right of the leader to exile," he said.

Apparently forcing himself to calm, Starscream snarled, "So be it. His will be a lonely existence."

"Not so much," Soundwave said. "Those who wish to follow the deposed may do so—also according to our tradition." He tore off his own badge. "I am no longer a Decepticon."

Listening to this as he walked away, Megatron smiled. Starscream was in for a rough night of leadership. Several more of the Decepticons were saying the same thing: Buzzsaw, Ravage, Spyglass, and Viewfinder. All of them threw their badges at the feet of Starscream, who was now sitting silent and angry.

And then the crushing blow came: a rumble from behind the throne. "My instincts tell me not to trust you," the voice said. "And I always trust my instincts." Unable to help himself, Megatron stopped walking and turned to see who else was leaving Starscream's fold. The giant warrior Omega Sentinel also tore off his badge, tossing it down to slam into the ground near Starscream. He stepped out from behind the throne.

"*What*?" Starscream said. "You can't! I reactivated you when Megatron would have left you in cold storage!"

Omega Sentinel leaned down, putting his massive face inches from Starscream. "I could wipe you out without straining a single circuit. I will not follow you—it's not logical." He turned and stepped past the other Decepticons milling about the throne.

Gleefully, Megatron turned back around and kept walking.

Behind him, those Decepticons who had chosen to leave turned to follow in Omega Sentinel's steps.

"Very well," Starscream yelled. "Just don't forget our other tradition…you are all forbidden from attacking me as well!"

"We have no need to attack you, Starscream," Megatron said, loud enough to be heard above the rumble of the moving Decepticons. "The Keepers will do that piece of work for us."

Without pausing, Megatron led his small band into the desert night. Once he reached the outskirts of the city, he followed Highway 95 south, to a little town called Searchlight, where he turned almost due west. They continued past the California border and into the Mojave National Preserve. He was long past the point where a safe conversation might be had, away from Starscream's prying spies, but he knew it would be better to be safe than sorry.

Finally, he stopped at a small campsite area and waited patiently for the others to join him. When everyone was gathered around, including the awesome Omega Sentinel, Megatron looked at them all with something bordering on genuine like.

"I'm pleased that you all have decided to abandon the traitor and follow me," he began. "You have made a wise decision."

"But now what?" Viewfinder said. "Why have you led us here?"

"Because here is where we will lay our plans for the future," Megatron said. "Starscream has desperately underestimated the power of the Keepers. For that failing alone, he will be destroyed."

"He has Devastator, and many others as well," Soundwave reminded him. "He is not without warriors."

"It will be no matter to the Keepers," Megatron said. "Their powers are vast."

"If so, then what will prevent them from destroying us, too?" growled Ravage, who was almost invisible in the dark.

"We must find a way to defeat them," Megatron stated calmly. "And in so doing, we will achieve everything I have long planned and hoped for."

"Then what is your plan, Megatron?" Soundwave asked.

"As of now," Megatron said, "the Keepers have given the inhabitants of the Earth three days to submit to their will. Undoubtedly, they will try to fight—even with the example of Los Angeles in front of them. Humans are not bright enough to surrender and try to fight another day. This serves us well. While the Keepers are distracted with the humans and Starscream, we will attack them in a way they would not expect."

A disgruntled snarl came from Ravage.

"How?" Megatron asked, understanding the snarl for what it was. "We will join forces with the Autobots."

The cacophony of protests was almost deafening.

"Megatron, we can't—" "Have you blown a—" "That's crazy—"

Megatron held up his hand for silence. "Listen to me, all of you. Done carefully and well, we will defeat the Keepers, the Autobots, and Starscream in one fell swoop. The Autobots are honor-bound to try and stop the Keepers, so we should help them by all means...provided that we conserve *most* of our strength and powers for when they are weakened. Starscream, too, will be in a difficult position.

"Once it becomes clear to those who stayed with him that the Keepers cannot be so easily defeated, he will begin to suffer defections and other problems—all while battling the Keepers, *trying* to be a new leader, and deal with an army of Autobots, along with ourselves, invading his territory."

Megatron laughed gleefully. "I used Optimus Prime to escape the Keepers' world, and I have no hesitation about using him again to defeat this menace...especially so long as it benefits me. Once the Keepers and Starscream are out of the way, our numbers will swell as the Decepticons who chose to remain with him revert their allegiance back to me. The Autobots, weakened from battle, will be easy to destroy. And then...all of the Earth and its resources shall be ours."

The assembled robots laughed and clapped at Megatron's plan. "But," he said, "we must move quickly. Starscream and the Autobots won't wait around for us. We need to move now if this plan has a chance of succeeding."

"How may we serve?" Soundwave asked.

"The first step is easy," Megatron said. "I need you to find my old friend Optimus Prime."

Soundwave looked around the gathered ex-Decepticons and nodded. "It shall be done," he said.

"Go, then," Megatron commanded. "Seek out the Autobot leader and tell him...."

"Yes?" Soundwave said.

"Tell him that I said I needed a favor," Megatron said. His laughter reached into the night sky, cold as iron in the arctic.

EIGHT

Paul and Melony had waited in the room for hours after Lomax finished questioning them. A uniformed officer who didn't bother to introduce himself brought them cold turkey and cheese sandwiches with steaming mugs of black, cop-shop coffee—neither of which were particularly good, but it beat nothing at all. Full night had come to the city. Paul imagined that even with the recent battles, the presence of the Keepers, and the presence of more Decepticons and Autobots than he'd even seen in one place before, there were still those who were sitting in a casino somewhere gamely plugging quarters and nickels and dimes into slot machines in the desperate hopes of making their fortune.

It was pointless, of course, but they did it anyway.

Not that Paul was unfamiliar with pointless activities. Years of being a police officer, first as a uniform, and then working his way through various roles as a detective, had provided him plenty of opportunities to do pointless things. Like arrest someone and see them back out on the street the next day.

Or question people who had done nothing wrong, and simply wanted to be on their way.

Paul could feel his frustration building. Melony, seated on one of the hard metal chairs next to him, fidgeted and sighed—she was probably just as bored and frustrated as he was. At least she'd stopped making passes at him. That had gotten very old, very fast. And after the Keepers had shown him the truth of her existence—that she was a Follower out of a strange cocktail of hate and guilt—he'd been determined to save her from herself. He wasn't completely certain why he felt this way.

It was almost two in the morning, by Paul's best estimation, when Lomax returned for them. He was followed by two uniformed officers. "Sorry about the wait," he said. "Some other matters took priority."

Paul nodded, staring hard at one of the uniformed officers—John Kelly. "That's fine," he said, rising to his feet. "Thanks for sending the food."

Melony, who had all the appearance of someone who had retreated into herself quite a ways, said nothing, but did stand.

"I've got to take you over to the Grand to be questioned," Lomax said. "Do I need to cuff the two of you, or will you play nice?"

Paul moved around the table. "Nice?" he asked.

"You won't make any trouble for me?" Lomax asked.

In two quick strides, Paul reached Officer Kelly, landing a solid blow to the officer's jaw. Kelly went down like a sack of oatmeal. Before the others could do more than shout, Paul stepped back and raised his hands. "No trouble at all," he said. "Now."

Lomax nodded, while the other officer helped the groggy Kelly rise to his feet. Behind them, Melony laughed. "Didn't see that one coming, did you?" she asked.

Kelly shook his head and spit blood. "What the hell was that for?" he mumbled.

"For hitting me with that tazer you've got built into your arm *after* I'd identified myself as a cop. You *could've* just asked me to come in with you," Paul said.

Lomax smirked. He was obviously a chief who didn't mind his subordinates being taken down a peg or two—even by an outsider.

Kelly wiped the blood off his lip and nodded. "Fair enough," he said. "But that's the only free one you get. Touch me again and I'll shove my arm up your backside and fire my tazer in places where you definitely *don't* want a shocking experience."

Paul grinned. "You could try," he said.

"All right, gentlemen," Lomax said, "that's enough." He turned to Paul. "Are you through?"

"I'm done," Paul said. "Let's get this finished."

Lomax nodded and motioned for Paul and Melony to precede them out the door. They walked down a hallway brightly lit with overhead fluorescents, and passed the desks where the on-duty cops filled out their paperwork.

They left the station house, climbed into an unmarked and obviously modified car. There were more bells and whistles on the dash than any police car he'd ever seen. Paul tapped Lomax, who was sitting in the front passenger seat, on the shoulder. "Looks like the Decepticons modified more than just your patrolmen," he said.

Lomax grunted an affirmative, then tapped the dashboard. "This is the kind of tech we could've had *years* ago, if we'd been willing to work with the Decepticons instead of against them. The engine's supercharged, won't overheat under most circumstances, and the vehicle itself has weapons and defense systems built into it."

"Pretty handy," Paul admitted.

"Oh yeah," Lomax said. "It's already kept several of our guys from being hurt during high speed chases and whatnot."

"Convenient," Paul said, then fell into silence. The car took them to the front lawn of the MGM Grand, where apparently Starscream had decided to put his headquarters.

As they crossed the lawn, Paul took note of how many Decepticons were present, and where they were positioned. He had no real idea of what Starscream wanted of him and Melony, but it was never a bad idea to have some sort of escape route in mind. That, and Paul remembered Starscream all too well....

Paul tumbled, the concrete below reaching up, ready to dash his brains, when a blur came and his fall was arrested, the breath knocked from his lungs as he struck something huge and metallic instead. He rocked back and forth, dazed, and realized he was still far above the ground, resting in Starscream's hand.

"Please," the priest said. "Put him down."

"I know mercy," Starscream said. "And forgiveness. If I close my hand, I might crush this being. Would you then offer me forgiveness?"

"If I believed you were truly aware of what you had done, that it had been wrong, that you had repented and were heartily sorry, yes. But if you take his life

simply to test my reaction, then no, forgiveness would not come to pass."

Paul looked out at the steel fingers, any of which might stab the life from him with blinding speed.

"Mercy, on the other hand, would be sparing the life of one I could destroy so easily, is that not so?" Starscream asked.

"Not entirely," the Father said. "If you spare him, it may be to gauge my reaction, to see what it benefits you. That is not mercy. Or you may set him down and let him run away as a sign of strength, to show you are beyond petty displays of power. Mercy is something one often grants one's enemies. and this boy is no threat to you."

The hand in which Paul had been cradled quickly sank to the ground, the fingers springing open like ramps the size of alligators. Paul raced to the ground, nearly passing out, but somehow managing, despite his terror, despite how numb he had become, to stumble onto the grass and wobble away from the Decepticon and the priest.

"He doesn't run," Starscream said.

"In his heart, he does," the Father said. "And, I fear, he always will."

Paul looked back. He had so much to say, so many questions to ask, but he was frozen. Somehow, he resisted the fear, and he spoke to the terrible machine. "I...I need to know...."

Starscream bent low. "Ask. One question."

"Paul," the Father warned, but it was too late.

Standing as still as he could, despite his fear, Paul asked, "Have you looked upon the face of God? Out there, in the emptiness, have you seen Him?"

Starscream laughed. "Only in my reflection, child."
The Father hung his head.

Paul, shattered, aware that he was being mocked, manipulated, stood trembling before the behemoth.

"BOO!" Starscream hollered.

Paul ran....

But that was a long time ago, Paul knew. Since then, he had given up his illusions about God, found satisfying and challenging work as a police officer, rather than the priest he had intended to be. He had put away bad guys. He had been in shoot-outs.

And he had been a prisoner of the Keepers.

Perhaps that, more than anything else, steeled his resolve to not break in front of Starscream as he had so long ago. And, though Paul remembered Starscream, it seemed doubtful that the Decepticon would remember the incident.

"Paul?" Melony said. "Are you all right?"

He nodded. "Fine," he said. "Just woolgathering, I suppose."

She shook her head in disbelief. "You picked a hell of a time for that."

Paul laughed. "Perhaps it was just my life flashing before my eyes."

Melony shuddered. "Let's hope not. I've seen enough death for awhile."

"Me, too," Paul said, thinking about how she'd snapped on the Keepers' world and tried to kill him.

They finished the trek across the lawn, weaving their way around the giant machines whose abilities, until recently, had seemed godlike to Paul. Lomax guided them to the foot of a gigantic, makeshift throne.

"Starscream?" he said. "The prisoners you wanted to question."

"Ah, yes," Starscream said. "Welcome." He gazed down upon the humans, a mechanical god of amazing powers…but Paul realized with a start that he was not afraid. Perhaps being saved by Megatron, riding in a giant's hand a second time, had cured him of his fear. Perhaps his experiences with the Keepers had moved him beyond anything resembling fright.

"What do you want with us?" Paul asked. "We have done nothing to warrant being your prisoner."

"You are absolutely correct," Starscream said. "An unfortunate choice of words on Chief Lomax's part, no doubt." He gestured to Lomax, who looked properly contrite. "You are not prisoners, but guests," he continued. "I wish only to hear what transpired on the Keepers' world."

"That would be a long and sad story," Paul said. "Mostly, they used us for amusement and entertainment."

"How so?"

"They would put us in different situations to watch our reactions, or they would make their prisoners battle each other to the death under nearly impossible circumstances. The Keepers were cruel and manipulative."

"I see," said Starscream. "And how powerful are they?"

Paul began to answer but Starscream held up his hand for silence. "Are they as powerful as we are? Do they rival us in technology?" He laughed. "Have *they* seen God's reflection in their mirrors?"

He remembers me! Paul thought. *Why?*

"I remember you, boy," Starscream said. "Though

humans do not age well. I saved your life and you asked me a question." He leaned forward on this throne. "Now answer mine."

"They are more powerful than any Decepticon I've ever seen," Paul said evenly. "Only Optimus Prime could defeat them and force them to return us to Earth."

"*Optimus Prime*?" Starscream screeched. "*I* am more powerful than Optimus Prime."

"I wouldn't know," Paul said. Greatly daring, he added, "Why do you remember me?"

"I know all about you, Detective Paul Chateris. I know the how's and why's of your life as well as you do—perhaps even more so." He waved a negligent hand as though shooing away a fly. "I even know about your pitiful organization called the Followers. Do we frighten you so badly? Is it not enough to know that *we* are your gods?"

"But why?" Paul asked. "Why should you care?"

"I don't," Starscream said. "But it's always good to know who you'd work with if the time came."

"Work with?"

"Look around you," Starscream said, waving a negligent hand. "Humans enjoying all the comforts our combined efforts can generate. I could use more Followers, but there's no longer any need to keep it a secret. I have work for you and yours."

Paul shook his head. "That's not for me to say," he said. "I just watch and file reports—and most of those are anonymous."

"Then send them a message," Starscream sneered. "Tell them that there's no longer a need to skulk about in the shadows. Come forth, learn about us…and in return, gain the knowledge of the universe you so desperately seek."

"Why?" Melony suddenly shouted. "You don't care about humans. They are worthless to you...to all of you!"

"Who is this person?" Starscream asked, his gaze flicking over the woman dispassionately.

"No one of importance," Paul said. He remembered his promise to himself to save Melony. Having Starscream's attention focused on her sent a shudder of fear down his spine.

"Melony Harcourt," she said. "You and your kind killed my sister." She spit on the ground. "If I had the power to do so, I'd take you apart with my bare hands."

As Starscream and the other Decepticons laughed, Paul said, "Being with the Keepers has unhinged her a bit. Pay her no attention."

"No attention?" Starscream asked. "You mean I should ignore an insult upon my person and my kind? A direct threat?"

"No, I—"

"Do you think I'm that *weak*?" shouted Starscream.

He leaped out of his throne, his giant form towering over the two of them. "Captain Lomax, take her away! She will be executed as an example to others."

Lomax immediately put her in handcuffs and began to march her off. Melony tried to fight, kicking and screaming, her black hair flying, but was quickly overcome by Lomax and his officers.

Paul tried to speak, but Starscream interrupted him again. "Say but one more word, *Follower*, and you will join her."

Paul's mouth shut immediately. He couldn't help her if he was dead.

"You will deliver my message to your organization," Starscream said. "If they know what's good for them, they'll join my cause. If not…they will be hunted down and destroyed!" He reseated himself. "Now get going!"

Paul turned and walked resolutely across the ground. Ahead of him, he could see Lomax shoving a shouting Melony into the same car they'd arrived in. He wondered how long he had to get her free before Starscream, who was obviously as mad as the proverbial hatter, made an example out of her and killed her.

And what *had* happened to Melony, exactly? While she was obviously a bit unstable when they were the Keepers' prisoners, she appeared rational enough. Now, it seemed like she'd totally come loose from her mental moorings. Perhaps when she'd tried to kill him, or perhaps when they'd gone through the gate, something had happened to her mind. It was hard to say.

As he walked down the street, Paul saw a church, and for the first time in many years, he considered stopping…not to pray for himself, but to pray for her. Underneath her hate and guilt, Paul believed she was a special person. She'd just been…damaged, like he had. But God, whoever or whatever or wherever he was, had little to do with the current situation.

The best Paul could do was walk on and try to find his own way.

But that didn't make the lonely walk into the Las Vegas night any shorter or easier. It took him a long time to find a phone that was working...and even longer to find the strength to begin making calls.

NINE

Allister Greaves was not a man who enjoyed waiting, so when the phone on his desk finally rang, he snatched it from its cradle, and snapped, "Greaves, and this had better be *someone* with news."

"Allister, is that the way a civilized man like yourself answers the phone?"

"I am *not* amused, *Agent* Franklin. What has kept you from reporting in for so long?"

"The usual things, Allister. You know, running for my life, dodging mortar rounds and rampaging Decepticons, trying to keep Spike Witwickey from guessing what's really going on, avoiding becoming a permanent guest of the Autobots....oh, and trying to figure out more about these so-called Keepers." Franklin's voice was almost chipper, which annoyed Allister even more.

Striving to keep his voice even, he said, "And what have you discovered?"

"Unfortunately, not a lot. But a couple of things are clear. First, even Optimus Prime acknowledges that the Keepers are far more powerful than the Transformers themselves. Second, Spike may look human, he may even act human, but he's got the knowledge we need buried in his mind—we just need to find a way to bring it out. And third, Las Vegas is a *very* dangerous place right now."

Allister stared thoughtfully at the muted television screen in front of him. Isolde Holden was offering another live report, though this one appeared to be in a much safer area. At least this time her cameraman didn't have to duck and dodge flying debris. He tapped his fingers lightly on the top of his mahogany desk.

"It appears quiet right now," he said.

"It's quiet now," Franklin said. "But I'm not completely sure why. Spike and the Autobots all took off when it became apparent that they were going to end up fighting some monstrous Decepticon Starscream found somewhere. I understand he's called Omega Sentinel, but where he came from, I don't know. Bumblebee was injured, and Prime wasn't in the greatest of condition either. Still, we know they've been willing to fight close battles in the past."

"Perhaps they left not because of the Decepticons, but because of the Keepers."

"It's likely," Franklin said. "All the data I've been able to access from here says that L.A. is totally gone behind some wall of black clouds. Nothing that goes in comes out."

"So I've heard," Allister said. "And what are the Decepticons doing?"

"That's what I've spent most of my time on," Franklin said. "Megatron has relinquished command of the Decepticons to Starscream and has left Las Vegas. A number of others—including that unknown titan—went with him. After that I saw something of real interest to us."

"And that would be?"

"Starscream questioned Paul Chateris and Melony Harcourt," Franklin said.

Allister ground his teeth together. Franklin had always had a touch of the dramatic, but to leave this information for the end of his report…. "Oh?" he said, striving for calm. "How did they end up with Starscream?"

"I don't know for sure," said Franklin. "Lomax brought them in, so they must have been taken by local cops sometime after crossing through the gate."

"Damn it to hell!" Allister said, his self-enforced calm snapping. "What the hell was Chateris thinking?"

"Obviously, he wasn't," said Franklin.

"So where are they now?"

"That's the best part. Melony is in custody—Starscream has sentenced her to death. Paul was let go. He has a message for us."

Allister sighed. "Go back to the beginning, if you please."

Franklin filled him in on what he had seen transpire between Starscream, Paul and Melony. "Basically," he concluded, "at least Starscream and his Decepticons know all about us. And probably the others with Megatron as well. But, they're willing to share their technology."

"It's no good, Franklin," Allister decided.

"Why not?"

"Because it's clear that Starscream is unstable in someway or another. And I daresay that Megatron may have bowed out for now, but he'll be back. The Decepticons are not to be trusted." He thought for a long moment, then added, "But that doesn't mean we can't use them, as they intend to use us."

Franklin laughed. "You play a dangerous game, Allister. Starscream and the other Decepticons are not easily fooled, nor should they be trifled with lightly."

"I, too, am dangerous, lest you forget it, Agent Franklin."

"How could I?" Franklin asked.

It had been Allister who had arranged for Franklin to receive the technological enhancements he now enjoyed, though his psyche profile had been borderline at best. Still, he was a good second, and his high placement with the NSA made him a valuable asset to the organization Allister had created. Franklin knew many, though not all, of Allister's secrets.

"Where's Chateris now?" he asked.

"He's down the street, about two blocks, using one of the few working pay phones in the city," Franklin said. "I can see him from here."

"Good," Allister said. "Pick him up and bring him in. I'll want to talk to Paul personally."

"What about Melony Harcourt?" Franklin asked.

Allister thought about the angry young woman. She'd proven a reliable witness in the past and he'd like to know her impressions of the Keepers. Still, she'd never been particularly stable.

"Can you get her out of the Las Vegas jail without there being an incident?"

"Unlikely," Franklin said. "They've got some heavy-duty tech floating around here these days."

Allister sighed, knowing when to cut his losses. "Very well, then. Leave her to her fate."

"You got it," Franklin said. "I'll bring Paul in by plane late tonight. Can you have a car there?"

"Of course," Allister said. "And Franklin?"

"Yes?"

"Don't frighten the man. I want him feeling cooperative."

"As you want it, Allister," Franklin said.

Allister hung up the phone and dialed a number. His driver answered on the first ring. "Yes, Mr. Greaves?"

"Take the car to our airport. Franklin will be coming in later tonight with a guest."

"Yes, sir," the man said, and disconnected.

His driver was a model of efficiency. If only all his other employees were as dedicated. Allister turned back to the television. Isolde Holden, a champion for the Autobots for quite some time, was gone. In her place was live streaming footage of the Keepers, huddled together on the lawn outside the Seven Wonders and More Casino.

While there was no doubt they looked horrible enough, and the idea that Bluestreak was somehow among them terrifying to most, what concerned Allister was that they appeared...*unconcerned*. They hadn't bothered to set up a defensive perimeter, there were no guards, nothing.

That meant they were either supremely confident in their ability to handle anything thrown at them, or they were supremely stupid.

Allister didn't think they were stupid.

Franklin walked calmly down the street to the phone booth where Paul Chateris was talking rapidly into a phone. The door was closed. Paul glanced at him, dismissed him, then turned back just as Franklin tapped on the glass.

Paul covered the mouthpiece of the receiver and said, "What do you want?"

"I want you to come with me, Paul," Franklin replied. "There's someone who'd very much like to meet you."

Paul slowly hung up the receiver, never taking his eyes off Franklin. He started to step out of the booth, but when Franklin didn't immediately move out of the way, he stopped. "How'd you know my name?"

Franklin smiled. If Paul had known more about him, the smile might have made him nervous. "We know *all* the names of our field operatives, Paul."

"Field operatives..." Paul said, his voice trailing off. "How did you find me so fast?"

"It was easy enough," Franklin lied smoothly. It was never a bad idea to make them think the organization had more eyes than it did. "We've been watching you ever since you came through the gate. This was our first chance to make contact."

"I'll say," Paul said, his eyes never leaving Franklin's. "But I'm feeling a bit distrustful tonight, so if it's all the same to you, I'll just phone in my report."

"I'm sorry," Franklin said, "that's not acceptable. You'll need to come with me now."

"*No*," Paul said. "Thanks, anyway."

"Paul, you're not getting me here," Franklin said, his voice turning cold. "You have a message to deliver, and we have a response to make. We'd like to go over it all with you *in person*." He edged closer to the door of the phone booth. "*Now*, do you get me?"

Paul nodded. "I get you."

"Good."

"How'd you know about the message?" Paul asked. Franklin smiled again. "I was listening," he said.

He motioned with his hand for Paul to step out of the booth. "I've acquired some transportation down the street. We'll be flying out tonight."

"Where?" Paul asked.

"You'll see when we get there," Franklin said.

"Fair enough. But I *really* need to check in with my day job. They probably think I'm dead."

"I'll take care of it on the way," Franklin said. "Let's get a move on. We don't want to keep the boss waiting. He's impatient about things like that."

Paul chuckled. "I just bet he is."

They walked down the street, Franklin slightly behind and to Paul's right. He'd done his best to keep the man calm, and it looked like things were going well, but if Paul decided to bolt, he'd knock him in the head and take him in unconscious…which was a distinct improvement over dead. It wasn't until he got in the car that Franklin remembered something quite important.

Spike had the crystal that called the Keepers and opened the doorway to this world.

Paul sat in the front passenger seat, staring into the desert night. The man who'd come for him appeared suddenly preoccupied and his facial expression ranged from mild consternation to that of a man suffering from severe gas pains.

"You didn't tell me your name," Paul said.

"No," the man said shortly. "I didn't."

"So what am I supposed to call you?"

"Call me Smith," he said. "John Smith."

"Ahh," Paul said. "The name of the famous Virginian, and common enough to be totally anonymous." He leaned back in his seat, searching for a comfortable position. For the first time, Paul realized how tired he was.

His companion grunted. "Anonymous is the name of the game."

"I bet," Paul said. "So, Mr. Smith, where are we headed?"

"A private airstrip about an hour west of here," he said.

Paul thought for a minute. "If you know about me, you must know about Melony."

"We do," he said shortly. "She's on her own."

"*What*?" Paul said. "You're just going to leave her there to die?"

The man nodded. "We're certainly not going to bash our way into the jail, create a huge scene, maybe get even more people killed, all so we can rescue one silly woman who didn't know how to keep her mouth shut."

"She's still one of the Followers," he said. "Isn't there something?"

"No," Smith said, his voice like ice. "There's not."

"What a fine group of people we are," Paul said. He stretched out in the seat, yawning and cracking his back. "You mind if I get some shuteye?"

Smith looked at him. "You're pretty calm for a guy who's seen what you've seen recently."

"No point in getting overly excited right now," Paul said. "And I haven't slept in days."

"Fair enough," he said. "I'll wake you when we get to the plane."

Paul nodded, and drifted into sleep, and almost immediately into dreams.

Once again, he saw Starscream save him from certain death, then mock him about God. He saw

Megatron save his and Melony's life.... Megatron, who also knew about the Followers...and wanted to learn more.

How had he found out about the Followers? And who, besides Starscream, also knew?

There was a traitor among them.

The plane was luxurious, though not ostentatious—leather seats, a self-serve minibar, and a pilot who didn't ask too many questions.

In fact, all he said to Smith was, "Where to, sir?"

To which he'd replied, "Omaha strip."

The pilot got into the plane and started it up while Paul and his anonymous companion seated themselves.

A long silence followed while the plane turned around and took off. Finally, Paul said, "You seem bothered by something."

Smith nodded. "I am," he said.

"Mind if I ask what?"

"Nothing too serious," he said, leaning his large bulk back into the seat. "Just the end of the world."

If he hadn't been so serious, Paul would've laughed. But given what he'd seen, the end of the world wasn't all that farfetched a notion.

The rest of the flight passed in silence, both men occupied with their own thoughts.

It was a long, dark night for them both.

TEN

Sunrise in the desert is a thing of grandeur. No casino façade with the best of intentions and technology can match it. The sun rose that morning over the mountains near Las Vegas, crossed the desert sands, and turned the entire sky a crimson color never matched by painters. Someone standing in the center of the Las Vegas Strip might have noticed that it was unnaturally quiet, but so long as there was power, the slot machines still made their electronic pitches for riches. And that wasn't the only noise of the awakening day.

The machines called Decepticons were also moving, several of them having been assigned by their mad leader Starscream to assess the damage, as well as ascertain the current position of the Keepers. Police patrol cars, enhanced by new technology, made rounds of the city, and began to slowly converge in a large radius around the Seven Wonders and More Casino, where the Keepers had been since arriving.

Periodic reports were sent to Starscream, who processed the information, and continued to finalize his plans.

Such as they were.

The Keepers were not unaware of these early morning developments. In point of fact, they had watched the living machine called Starscream with great interest. After issuing their warning and displaying their power, they had spent the long night rapidly devouring knowledge of this world and its inhabitants. Their minds were linked with one another, a communally shared intelligence, but with individual personalities. The Keepers were not required to share information with each other, but they found the technique useful when knowledge of a place might help them as a whole or as individuals.

The Keeper who had identified himself as The Voice expressed their conclusions in the vaults of their nearly limitless minds. It wasn't speech as humans know it, but thought expressed as such. *"The one called Starscream is...broken somehow. He is mad for power, but the data shows he is not unintelligent. Something has gone wrong with him. He will not heed our warning to submit, and those who follow him will also attempt to fight. They must be destroyed."*

The Keeper who had once been called Bluestreak disagreed. *"They must not be destroyed. They must be captured and taken over, like this one. Their bodies make formidable weapons. Once contained, we can use them to destroy the others who have left.... Optimus Prime, who harmed us so grievously and Megatron who betrayed us."*

The Keepers mentally chewed on this idea for several seconds. A chorus of voices responded. *"How?"*

The former Bluestreak, who knew much about the Decepticons before the Keepers had contained him, provided the information. *"The one called Starscream has a weakness for human customs. I will approach him under a flag of truce and contain him."*

"And the others? Those moving into place even now?"

"They will not act without an order from Starscream. An order that will not be forthcoming."

The Keepers conferred within their minds, discussed, dissected and decided what their actions would be. *"It is decided. Go and acquire this Starscream. The others will soon follow."*

Bluestreak stood and left the group, pausing only long enough to slam a fist through the wall of the casino and remove a sheet from the bed. The signal for a truce... that it should be a white sheet from a bed, the same color as what often lined coffins, seemed perfectly appropriate. Once contained in a Keeper's mind, the body was gone forever.

Trapped inside his own body, buried so deep that there was no light, Bluestreak tried to keep himself from screaming. No one would hear him anyway. For what seemed like days and days, he had tried everything he could think of to take control of himself, but every doorway to his essential functions was as sealed off as he and Prime had been on the Keepers' world.

Bluestreak could remember fighting with Jazz, trying to avoid killing each other or the human spectators, until it became clear that one of the two Autobots would have to die for it to end....

He rolled to a stop just in front of the humans, one of whom bolted, sprinting away from him and toward the awful tentacles that would mean certain death. Knowing it would give Jazz an opening he could ill afford to pass up, Bluestreak still lunged forward, try-

ing to put himself between the human and the tentacles....

Golden fire...the energy from Jazz's photon weapon seared through his back like heat from a burning star. Bluestreak felt himself lifted, propelled into the air and then dropped as the beams punched through his chest. Hitting the floor of the arena with a resounding crash....

Jazz moved the terrified—but very much alive—human to safety, then rolled Bluestreak over.

He asked if they were safe and made Jazz promise to kill Megatron....

The Keepers demanded that the victory be completed, and Bluestreak knew what Jazz had to do. "Do it," he tried to say, but it came out a stutter. "You needed to win," he added, though this statement, too, came out garbled.

Jazz stood and placed his rifle next to the gaping wound in his chest...and fired.

Then, all was darkness....

When he awoke, the darkness had not receded, but there was no pain. He tried to feel for his arms, his legs, his head, but there was nothing. He was a consciousness trapped in his own body. Bluestreak remembered reading an article that speculated about human coma patients being locked within their own minds, unable to feel or act, their thoughts the only company they had.

But he was also aware of what transpired around him. Bluestreak could hear and see, but he had no more control over his own body or his actions than did one who was dead.

In some ways, he wished he were.

But he was not one to give up hope that easily. Optimus had once told him that a warrior's spirit comes from within; if that was true, he was about as within as one could get. He *owed* the Keepers for what they had forced Jazz to do. He *owed* Megatron.

If there was an escape, a way to take control over the tiniest piece of himself, Bluestreak would find it…and then, finally, there would be justice.

The Keeper who inhabited Bluestreak's now modified body knew of his struggles to get out of the mental prison into which he'd been placed. It would have been easy enough to simply douse the small flicker of life left in the body and then use it for their own ends, but the Keepers enjoyed seeing how a conscious life form reacted in this type of prison as much as any other. The Keeper had no real name, nor any designation. He felt no need for one. He simply was.

The entity called Bluestreak, however, still called itself that—even without form, it insisted on at least the mental semblance of what it had once been. Its attempts to free itself had been amusing so far. Later, he would relay the information to the other Keepers. They would find its, he was certain, fascinating.

For now, though, he had more important things to take care of. He held the sheet aloft, and marched down the street. He was not challenged or stopped, but he detected many life forms, including those who called themselves Decepticons nearby. Several followed closely. Their conversations and even their thoughts were open to him.

Bluestreak was known as an Autobot, but his form had been drastically altered to accommodate the

Keeper. At first, this was what slowed response to his presence more than anything else. On a high-range frequency, the Decepticon called Starscream was warned of his impending presence.

Starscream indicated that, by all means, they should let him come.

If the Keeper had been capable of such an expression, he might have smiled at this foolish course of action. Instead, he simply kept walking, holding the sheet up like a flag fluttering in the grip of a giant standard-bearer.

By the time he reached the MGM Grand, several other Decepticons had joined their leader. A force of humans, bedecked in some type of combat gear, had stationed themselves on the perimeter of the lawn, apparently prepared to do battle in defense of this mad machine.

The Keeper stalked across the lawn, ignoring the others, the movement of his body the only real noise in the quiet landscape. He stopped in front of Starscream's throne, reviewing all he and the others had been able to learn about human customs of this nature. He inclined his head, but did not kneel.

"I have come under a banner of peace," the Keeper said. Its voice was similar to Bluestreak's, but more grinding, as though his vocal apparatus had new gears in it.

"So I see," said Starscream. "To what do I owe the pleasure of your visit?"

"I have come to ask you to surrender. *You* will be taken into custody, your human combat forces dispersed. Your companion Decepticons will be allowed to leave."

Starscream's high-pitched laugh spiraled into the

sky. "Oh my," he said, glancing at the other Decepticons nearby. "I'm going to be arrested."

"Yes," the Keeper said. "In a manner of speaking."

"You're very brave to come here," Starscream sneered. "Even now, I have your position surrounded. Very shortly, I will have my forces attack and wipe you off the face of the Earth."

"You make assumptions based on knowledge you do not possess," the Keeper said. "We are more than capable of destroying you, as you might an insignificant insect. We are equally capable of wiping out this entire planet."

Starscream looked at his gathered forces and smiled. "I think you made a mistake in coming here. You look and even sound a bit like Bluestreak, but I'm certain that even one as cowardly as he would strike you down in an instant. *We* are not weakling humans. *We* are masters of the universe!" As he concluded his statement, Starscream reached out with his massive hand to shove the Keeper backwards.

The instant his hand made contact with the creature, however, he froze in stasis. "You are incorrect," the Keeper said. "It is *you* who made the mistake...in allowing *me* to get this close to you." A bolt of bluish-purple energy leapt from the Keeper's hand to slam into the immobile Starscream. While his paralysis kept him from defending himself, it did allow him to jerk and writhe and even utter a high-pitched scream as the energy worked its way through his armor.

The other Decepticons tried to jump into the fray, only to slam into an invisible wall of force surrounding the Keeper and Starscream. They pummeled at it uselessly, even fired their energy weapons at it to no effect. The human forces took up the idea and also began firing.

The Keeper was pleased. The others had ensured his safety by placing the field around him as soon as Starscream was within range. The Keeper fired another energy bolt into the writhing robot at his feet. A quick survey showed that Starscream's circuits were close to overload.

On the ground, Starscream jerked and quivered and raged, but was unable to rise to his feet. The Keeper looked at the other Decepticons. "You would be wise to depart," he said. "To continue on this course of action is folly. Surrender and live. Leave this place." He looked at the stricken mechanical giant at his feet, and the thought briefly crossed his mind that it would make a fine body for one of his brethren.

"Or stay," he added, "and join him in death." He fired another bolt into Starscream's chest—a sizzling crackle of energy and power that caused smoke and sparks to erupt from underneath the armor plating that protected his vital systems. Several seconds passed, and as the power left Starscream's limbs, the brief light of sanity shone in his eyes.

"R...run...you...fools," he stuttered. His eyes went dark.

The Decepticon called Skywarp had begun powering up his primary weapon, but seeing Starscream so effectively terminated apparently caused him to rethink his actions. He stepped back and looked at the other Decepticons. "Retreat," he said, broadcasting his command to all the forces listening. It was the only logical thing for them to do.

He turned and fired his thrusters, heading for the outskirts of the city. The others, both those close by and those who had been watching the Keepers, turned almost as one and fled in the same direction.

They had just cleared the last of the buildings when the Keepers took the final step in their plan. A net of energy surrounded the fleeing machines, swatting some out of the sky and driving others to the ground.

Skywarp climbed to his feet. "You said you'd let us go," he said to no one in particular.

The altered voice of Bluestreak answered. "We lied."

The former Autobot grabbed the form of the fallen Starscream, turned, and began dragging him back to the other Keepers. One of them was about to get a new body.

Bluestreak was torn between rejoicing when Starscream was struck down and terror at the realization that these beings were so powerful that even the mighty Starscream had fallen before them. Devastator himself had tried to break through the energy barrier. Over sixty feet tall and able to knock down a concrete bridge with one blow, he had no more effect on it than the buzzing of a fly.

The Keepers, Bluestreak realized, represented more danger to Earth than all the battles between the Autobots and the Decepticons combined. This world would be ravaged just like his, Cyberton, had been—a smoking ruin, where death and destruction covered the horizon as far as the eye could see.

Once again, Bluestreak turned his efforts to finding a way to escape his prison. If he could find the tiniest crack, the smallest seam...he would find a way to squeeze through. And then he'd wring the very life from this evil creature that held him.

Somehow.

CHAPTER

ELEVEN

Hello, Optimus! Hello, Spike!" Bumblebee called cheerfully.

Optimus and Spike turned to see the little yellow robot walk toward them. He had obviously been restored to full functionality—something that made Prime profoundly grateful. He had learned to count on Bumblebee's optimistic attitude for shoring up the other Autobots when times were tough.

As they were now.

"So, what's happening?" Bumblebee asked. "Anything new?"

"I've sent Wheeljack to have a look around," Prime said. "He's glad to be back in action again. But it's clear that we have major problems ahead of us." He turned to Spike and nodded. "Show him."

From his jacket pocket, Spike carefully withdrew a bluish-white crystal. Strange, pulsating marks lined its surface.

"Whoa!" Bumblebee said. "What is that?"

"It's…some kind of communications device," Spike said. "It's also what opened the gate to this world and allowed Optimus and the others to return here." He thought for a moment, then added ruefully, "Of course, it also allowed the Keepers to come through, too. I didn't really intend for that to happen."

"You mean *you* activated this device?" Bumblebee asked.

Spike shook his head. "Nothing so purposeful, I'm afraid. I just..." Spike's voice trailed off.

"Guessed," Prime said. "And it worked."

"So you could use it to open the gate again," Bumblebee said, "and send the Keepers right back to where they came from!"

"I wish it were that easy," Spike said, "but I don't think it works that way. Prime and I have been up most of the night talking about it. I think someone here activated the device the first time and allowed the Keepers enough time to grab Optimus and Megatron, along with all those people in Tokyo. That someone wasn't me, but whoever it was, they obviously know a lot more about this thing than I do."

"Then how'd you figure it out?" Bumblebee asked.

"Like Optimus said—I mostly guessed."

Prime thought for a minute about his old friend Spike. "I think maybe you know more than you think you do, Spike. How much do you remember of being an Autobot?"

Spike sighed. "More than I thought, apparently," he said. "Franklin and several others seem to believe that they can somehow...pry the data out of my mind and by doing so learn all about how Autobots are built, what they think, even how to turn a human into one."

"That type of knowledge is not something the human race is ready for, I'm afraid," Prime said. "That's why what Starscream has done in Las Vegas is so wrong. Technology should be earned with equal parts responsibility and compassion. Humans are too emotional to handle the kinds of technology that Starscream has given to them. It's much like the augments—like your friend Franklin. Given time, humans could learn to handle such things, but not yet."

"Optimus," Spike said, "for a short time, I was one of you. While I don't remember all that much, I do know one thing: you have our best interests at heart, and you'd never intentionally do anything to hurt us."

"I appreciate your faith in me, my friend," Optimus said. "I wish it were shared by more of the people on Earth. But it's not, and the information you carry buried in your memory must be protected at all costs."

Spike nodded, then turned as Wheeljack entered the room, almost running.

"You're never going to believe this!" he said, sliding to a stop in front of Optimus.

"Now what?" Prime said.

"Soundwave is on his way here…or at least to this general area. I overflew him on the road—you should have seen his face!—and he called for a parley. I figured what the heck and stopped. He says he's come with a message from Megatron. He says that Megatron wants to ask you a favor." Wheeljack laughed. "Like you'd ever grant him a favor!"

Spike and Bumblebee joined in the laughter until all three noticed that Prime wasn't laughing.

"Very well," Prime said, getting to his feet. His voice was resigned, but firm. "Where is Soundwave now?"

Waiting near the road where he had talked with Wheeljack, Soundwave watched the approaching Autobots with care. While they weren't known for treachery, it always paid to be cautious. Too many fights between them all.

The last few days had been…interesting. While his plan to see Starscream humiliated in front of Megatron had failed, there had been moments of pure satisfaction—not the least of which was seeing Megatron use Starscream's own supposed values to walk off with a number of Decepticons and begin his plans for vengeance.

He had deduced who had summoned the Keepers originally—though that person had been duped into believing they could be controlled. He even knew that Spike was the one mostly responsible for bringing them, along with Megatron and Optimus Prime, back to this world. What he wasn't sure of was how. And as soon as he knew that, he would act to wrest that power away and offer it up to Megatron. Now that Megatron and Starscream had gone their separate ways, Megatron would need a new second-in-command, and Soundwave fully intended that it be him.

Coming to a stop in front of him was Optimus Prime, the annoying chatterbox Bumblebee, Prowl and Wheeljack. Likely, they had spirited the human Spike away to some *relatively* safe corner of the world.

"Soundwave," Optimus said, not bothering with pleasantries. "You have a message for me?"

"Indeed," Soundwave said, crossing his arms over his blue-and-white chestplate. "Megatron wished me to convey to you that he requests a favor."

"Very well," Optimus said. "I will accompany you to him."

Soundwave started in surprise. He hadn't really believed that Optimus would do more than send him back with a curt reply when Megatron had sent him to deliver this message. Since when did Optimus Prime come running when Megatron called?

Optimus turned to the others. "You will return to base," he said. "When I get back, I will want your ideas on how to dislodge the Keepers from this world."

"Wait just a darn minute, Optimus!" Prowl said. "You're not seriously thinking of going off to face Megatron alone, are you?"

"I am *not* thinking about it," Prime said. "I'm doing it. I won't have you and the others put at risk. Nor am I 'facing' Megatron as you put it. I am rendering a favor to him, which would be hard to do if he killed me right out of the gate."

"But!" "Hold on!" and a chorus of other exclamations followed, but the Autobots fell immediately silent when Optimus raised his hand. Soundwave had to admit to himself that Optimus' commanding presence impressed him. He led his troops well.

"Enough," Optimus said. "You have your orders." He turned to Soundwave. "Which way?"

Soundwave gestured back down the highway. "Follow me," he said.

The two of them started down the road, and Soundwave wondered why Optimus was being so cooperative. He also wondered if maybe this was some kind of trick.

Optimus Prime arrived in the clearing occupied by Megatron and the other Decepticons who had left Las Vegas with him. He came alone, not because he was unafraid that this might be a plot of some kind, but because he knew the importance of an alliance between them. Only together could they hope to defeat the Keepers.

Megatron turned to face him, and Optimus immediately sensed that Megatron had reached the same conclusion. For a long moment, the two enemies stared at each other. Their alliance on the Keepers' world had been necessitated by the situation; would they be able to put aside their differences for a while longer? "Megatron," he said. "You requested a favor, and here I am—as promised."

The assembled Decepticons mumbled quietly at this revelation, but said little.

"Optimus," Megatron said. "I am pleased that you remember our bargain back on the Keepers' world."

"How could I forget?"

"Not easily, I would imagine," Megatron said. "You lost one of your Autobots there, didn't you? Bluestreak, as I recall."

"Your memory is correct," Optimus said. "Bluestreak was killed, his body taken over by the Keepers."

"That must gall you," Megatron said.

"Almost as much as having to surrender command of the Decepticons to Starscream must have galled you," Optimus replied.

A grimace crossed Megatron's features. "Indeed," he said. "But enough sparring. I asked you here to propose—"

"An alliance," Optimus interrupted.

"Yes," Megatron said. "I see we've both reached the same conclusion."

"We have," Optimus said. "The only way to get rid of the Keepers is to destroy them. And the only way to do that is if we team up. Even then it will be...difficult."

"But not impossible," Megatron said. "You have the Matrix. That hurt them before."

"That was on their world," Prime said. "What powers they have here, what defensive abilities, I do not know."

"Formidable ones, I would imagine," Megatron said. "You have heard about Los Angeles?"

"Yes," Optimus said. "We've heard the reports." He looked at the assembled Decepticons. "How do your forces feel about an alliance?"

"*Feel*?" Megatron asked. "Their feelings are inconsequential. They will do as I command because they trust in my abilities."

"An interesting approach," Optimus said. "But different than mine. I will need to discuss this with my Autobots."

"I was sure you would," Megatron said.

Optimus reviewed the conversation in his head. "Is this alliance the favor you would have of me?" he asked.

"No," Megatron said, "but I feared that you would ignore a general summons. You and I both know that this is mutually necessary." He looked at Optimus carefully. "Favors are not done of mutual necessity. I'll save that one for another day."

"I'm sure you will," Optimus said. He looked once more around the forested clearing. "You've chosen an odd place for your new headquarters."

"Temporary, I assure you," Megatron said. "We'll be returning to our usual headquarters when all of this is done." He paused for a moment, looking around the rustic clearing. "Starscream may well be insane, but his idea of working *with* the humans wasn't completely bad. At least his quarters are more comfortable."

Soundwave, who had remained silent through most of this, suddenly jerked his head in surprise, then smiled evilly. "I doubt that's the case now," he said.

"What do you mean?" Megatron asked.

"I just picked up a transmission out of Las Vegas—a plea for assistance."

"From who?" Megatron asked.

"Skywarp, believe it or not," Soundwave said. "Shall I play it back for you?"

"Yes!" Megatron said. "Don't stand there like a dolt, let's hear it!"

"Very well," Soundwave said, then began to play the message: "Megatron or any other Decepticon within range.... Starscream has been destroyed by the Keepers.... We are trying to escape...an energy field of some type...." Then the message went to static.

"I'd say things have turned for the worse for those who chose to stay with the traitorous Starscream," Megatron said. "But I wish they hadn't robbed me of the opportunity to kill him myself."

"There will be plenty of death before this battle is through," Optimus said. "I must go now and discuss this alliance with the Autobots. Where will I find you?"

Megatron gestured to the clearing. "Right here," he said. "I find it more to my liking than Las Vegas right now."

"I'm sure you do," Optimus said. "I will return shortly with our answer."

Optimus turned and left the clearing, heading back the way he'd come. The alliance was necessary, though distasteful. And there was no doubt in his mind that Megatron had one scheme or another up his metallic sleeve. He knew that Megatron wouldn't rest until his revenge on the Keepers, and on those Decepticons who had betrayed him, was complete.

And whatever he chose to call his favor would likely cost Optimus everything he valued...and possibly much more.

CHAPTER

TWELVE

Allister Greaves didn't sleep much. For the most part, he found it to be an irritating necessity, and he could function very well on two or three hours of sleep each night. Some nights, he slept not at all. He could do this for several days before requiring rest, and on those nights, he would sleep six hours and no more. To do otherwise was to invite a headache of massive proportions.

While he was waiting for Franklin to bring Paul in, he chose to continue monitoring data and making assessments. It was early morning, and his driver had just called to say that the plane had arrived when Isolde Holden burst onto the air with the news.

"It is another morning here in the decimated city of Las Vegas. Yesterday began with a fierce battle between the Decepticon known as Starscream and a handful of defiant Autobots led by none other than the fearsome Grimlock. That battle continued on and off throughout the day as both human and Transformer forces tried to control the city.

"During the height of the afternoon, a strange rift appeared in the sky. Some say it was a gate to another world. What is known is that the Trans-

formers and many of the humans who had disappeared so mysteriously in Tokyo stepped through the
gate…but they were not alone.

"Also coming with them were numerous alien life
forms, many of which died when they were unable
to adapt to our environment. One group of the aliens,
however, appears to have adapted quite readily to
our world, but in the most hostile and terrifying of
ways.

"They call themselves the Keepers, and yesterday
they issued an ultimatum requiring that all the
inhabitants of the Earth surrender and submit to their
will…or suffer the consequences. As a demonstration
of their power, they have—apparently—destroyed the
city of Los Angeles. This morning, they have demon-
strated their power once again.

"Under a flag of truce, one of the Keepers, who has
somehow melded his own body and that of the presumed dead Autobot Bluestreak, approached
Starscream. By all reports we've been able to gather,
Megatron has surrendered his leadership of the
Decepticons to Starscream and departed with a
handful of the others. Those that remained, including
Skywarp and the massive Devastator, were present
when the Keeper approached and ordered Starscream
to surrender himself.

"Starscream refused, and the Keeper retaliated in
the harshest of manners. One police officer I spoke
to said that the Keeper used some form of electro-
paralysis combined with an energy weapon that destroyed Starscream in a matter of a few short minutes."

Allister, who had been tuning out the useless
information from the day before suddenly sat up
straight in his chair. Had he heard that correctly?

"I can confirm that I personally saw the body of Starscream being dragged down the Las Vegas Strip and into the lawn area of the Seven Wonders Casino. There are also reports that the other Decepticons who were present here have also been captured and are being held by the Keepers somewhere outside the city."

Starscream dead? The Decepticons with him captured? Just how powerful were these beings? Allister wondered.

"At present, the remaining citizens of Las Vegas, and even the rest of the world, must wonder at this development. What will our government's reaction be? What must it be? And where are the Autobots, who have so often been maligned in the media, but have so often saved us from ourselves?

"This is Isolde Holden, reporting live from Las Vegas."

Allister glanced at his watch and picked up the phone. He dialed Elisa's number from memory. Even though it was quite early in the day, she answered immediately. No accent this time, just business. "Hello, Mr. Greaves," she said.

"Elisa, what's going on out there?" Allister demanded. "What are they doing?"

"The only thing they can do," she said. "They're mobilizing an attack force, though they're not holding out a lot of hope."

Allister could hear in her voice that she was holding something back. "What else, Elisa?"

"The talk is that they'll only risk one shot at the Keepers before going to other methods."

"Such as?" Allister said, fearing he knew the answer. America was extremely predictable in its response to threats against it, and the current sitting President even more so.

"I've heard them talking about utilizing nukes," she said, her voice just barely above a whisper. "No one wants to, but nuclear is nothing compared to what these beings did to L.A."

A good point, Allister thought. "What kind of troops are they sending?"

"They're planning a series of air strikes, followed by Special Forces ground troops. The word has gone out very quietly to the media people and as many residents as could reach to get the hell out of there. The local police, as confused as they currently are with Starscream out of the picture, have also been notified. No one here thinks it will work."

Allister stared at the images on the television screen—a newscast repeat of the footage from yesterday. "I don't either," he said finally. "When are they going?"

"I don't know for sure," she said. "I'll try to find out."

"I appreciate it, Elisa," Allister said.

"Mr. Greaves?" she said. "Get our people out of there if you can."

"I'm going to try, Elisa," he said, knowing that it was all but impossible. "I'll try." He broke the connection and turned his attention back to the reports on his desk. His mind, disciplined to multi-tasking, listened to the occasional report on his earpiece, while he visually looked at data in printed form.

Three-quarters of an hour later, a chime sounded, notifying him that Franklin and Paul had arrived. He went to meet them. There was a great deal to do.

Franklin and Paul got out of the car, a black stretch limo that had met them on a deserted airstrip about fifty miles northwest of Omaha. Paul had slept off and on throughout the long flight, but Franklin had chosen to stay awake. Since he'd been augmented, his need for sleep was significantly less than it had been. Of course, Greaves didn't sleep much either, and he wasn't an augment...he was just focused. The drive over had been another hour and a half, over winding dirt roads and past rolling cornfields so green it was almost tropical in color. Unless you had a compass in your head, it would be damn hard to know exactly where you were. Everything out here looked the same—until they drove over one more hill and the estate of Allister Greaves appeared.

The grounds and the house were immaculate, and every time Franklin visited here, he felt a small worm of envy for Allister's lifestyle. The man was extraordinarily wealthy, though where all that money came from was difficult to say. No doubt a good portion of it came from Allister's inventions, of which there were many. It had been Allister who'd created the initial technology to create augments like himself.

The leader of the Followers opened the door and stepped into the early morning sunlight. As always, he was immaculately dressed in a suit and tie, his wolf's head cane at his side. "Good morning, gentlemen," he said. "I trust the flight was comfortable."

"A little long," Franklin said, "but we managed." He nudged Paul. "He slept most of the time."

Allister took a long moment, obviously studying the man. "You seem calm," he noted.

Paul looked around the grounds and turned to Allister. "There's little point in expending a lot of extra energy getting overly excited. Given what I've seen and heard over the last few days, a mansion in Nebraska is hardly mind-boggling."

Allister laughed. "I suppose you're right at that, Paul." He turned back to Franklin. "What name did you give him?"

"John Smith," Franklin said with an indifferent shrug.

"Not particularly inventive," his boss noted. "But it will suffice."

"And you are?" Paul asked.

"Allister Greaves," he said, holding out his hand. "I founded the Followers."

Paul's eyes widened a bit. "*The* Allister Greaves?" he asked, shaking hands. "I heard you were dead."

Allister laughed again. "I've heard that a few times myself."

"You invented the math and language implant chips the government was drooling over a few years ago. The human rights groups had a field day. I remember it well."

"Yes, they did," he said. "But we've got more important things to discuss right now." He turned back to Franklin. "Have you gotten any updated reports out of Vegas this morning?"

"No," the agent said. "I figured I'd update myself when I got here. Why? What's happening?"

"Come inside, gentlemen," Allister said. "We'll have some coffee and then I'll bring you both up to date on how Starscream got himself killed first thing this morning." He turned and went back into the house without so much as a backwards glance.

Franklin, trying not to choke in his surprise, muttered, "He loves to do that. Throw terribly important information at you like it was nothing." He started into the house, motioning for Paul to follow him. "I *hate* it when he does that. Just hate it."

Paul followed the man who called himself John Smith into the mansion. The news that Starscream had been destroyed was...difficult to grasp. He'd been sent here by Starscream to ask for the Followers to come and *be* Followers. Instead, he wondered what his purpose would now be.

The inside was as beautiful and immaculate as the outside. Dark walls of real wood lined both sides of a long hallway that, by all appearances, ran all the way to the back of the structure. Original oils, an eclectic mix of portraits and landscapes, hung on the walls. The carpet runner on the floor had the look of a Persian, and Paul had no doubts that it was real. He followed the two men, once glimpsing a massive dining room and another time a library that would have been the envy of many public schools.

They finally turned right and went into a room that was clearly a study of some sort, though not what Paul would have imagined. A bank of televisions lined one wall, all of them on, though the volume on each had been muted. On one side of the room, a small conference table made of some type of granite or marble was surrounded by four, heavily padded work chairs. In the center of the table, a rotating computer screen and communications module was dark and silent, though Paul guessed it could be up and running in nanoseconds. On the other side of the room, a massive mahogany desk with a burgundy-colored leather chair dominated the scene. On the desk were neatly organized stacks of paper—reports, no doubt—and behind it, a wall of shelves filled with books of some sort.

To one side of the conference table, a small rolling cart had been set up. "In anticipation of your arrival," Allister said, "I've had a light breakfast prepared."

Paul, who hadn't eaten anything of real nutritional value in quite some time, stepped forward. "I don't mean to be rude," he said, "but to be perfectly honest, I'm famished." He opened the metal lid on the cart and examined the contents with mounting pleasure.

Freshly brewed coffee and just-squeezed orange juice were side-by-side, while a selection of sweet pastries was interspersed with cut-up pieces of cantaloupe, pineapple, banana, and grapes. In a heated round, sausage and bacon were being kept warm next to a tin of scrambled eggs. Lightly toasted English muffins rounded out the offerings. Paul snared a plate off the cart, along with silverware and a napkin, then helped himself. Smith was close behind. Both men chose coffee over the juice.

When he noticed that Allister hadn't gotten anything for himself, Paul said, "You're not joining us?"

Allister smiled. "No, thank you for asking. I've already had my breakfast."

"You must be an early riser," Paul noted.

"Something like that," Allister agreed, then motioned for them to sit at the conference table.

The men ate quickly and in silence. Allister didn't interrupt their meal with questions, for which Paul was profoundly grateful. Other than the sorry meal he'd been served in the Las Vegas jail, he hadn't really eaten since returning from the Keepers' world...and he had a suspicion that all of the sustenance he'd had there was enhanced by the Keepers' powers, and not real food at all.

After they finished, Allister rang for a servant, who entered the room and cleared the dishes away with a minimum of fuss. He did, however, leave the coffee. When he left, Allister turned to Paul. "I suspect that Starscream's death leaves you at a bit of loose ends. He'd sent you here asking, or rather demanding that we—that is the Followers—present ourselves to him. Now he's dead and those Decepticons who stayed with him are in the Keepers' power."

"That about sums it up," Paul agreed. "Which, I guess means I'm free to go on about my business."

"Not exactly," Allister said. He revealed the government's plan to launch an assault on the Keepers.

"Holy hell!" Paul said. "That's going to be a bloodbath! Don't those people realize how dangerous these beings are?"

"Likely they do," he said, "but what choice do they have? They cannot just surrender to them without a fight."

"So what would you have me do?" Paul asked. "At this moment, I'm probably presumed dead by my department back home, or if not, at least unemployed."

Allister looked at Smith, who nodded an affirmative. "Actually, that matter was taken care of last night while you slept. An extended leave has been arranged for you—with pay, I might add—and your chief knows you are safe."

"How'd you—" Paul tried to say, but Smith shook his head.

"Don't worry about it," he said. "One of the many services I am able to provide."

"Convenient," Paul said. "I should've told you to get me a raise while you were at it." He turned his attention back to Allister. "So, now what do we do?" he asked.

"The only thing we *can* do," Allister said. "We're going to pull our people out of Vegas, fast as we can. In the meantime, I'll have others working on other things—like helping the government get some better information than they have now."

"And how do I fit into all this?" Paul asked.

"Simple," Allister said. "You're going to be the one who gets our people out of town. Starting with your companion from the Keepers' world."

"But Smith here said that—"

"Plans change, Paul," the man said. "One of the things required of a leader is adaptability. The mission of the Followers is to learn about the Transformers. These Keepers are a threat to that, and to everyone on this planet. Before, it would have been a foolish risk to try and rescue Melony from Starscream. Now that he's dead, and the other Decepticons out of the way, it's a safe bet to assume that the Keepers have better things to worry about than a handful of humans interested in the Transformers."

Paul nodded. "I suppose you're right about that, anyway," he said. "But how am I going to get her, let alone the others, out of Las Vegas?"

"You'll be given the resources necessary for your mission."

The man who called himself Smith cleared his throat. "And what about me?" he asked.

"You have a different task," Allister said. "You're going to go find Optimus Prime and tell him that we want to help."

"He doesn't trust me," Smith said. "What makes you think he'll even talk to me?"

"That, too, is simple. If he doesn't want to make a deal, explain about Spike's family and what will happen to them if cooperation isn't immediately forthcoming." Allister's voice had grown soft and cold as he spoke, an arctic wind from a man used to getting his way.

"You're the boss," Smith said. He stood and motioned for Paul to do the same. "I suppose we'd better get going. I'll drop you off at the airstrip."

"You'll have the resources you need by the time you reach the plane, Paul," Allister said. "Don't fail me—or them."

"I won't," Paul said, thinking of Melony. If he could save her, could show her that random chance had more to do with her sister's death than the Transformers, maybe she could let go of her hate and guilt. He would undertake this mission—but not for the Followers, who he had come to recognize as something a great deal more organized than a cult. For himself. A chance at personal redemption, even if his soul was long since lost.

"Excellent," Allister said. Then he turned back to Smith. "I want *regular* reports from you from here on in."

Smith grinned. "Of course," he said. "Have I ever failed you before?"

Allister didn't bother to answer, and the two men left the mansion together, neither one knowing of the secrets the other carried in his heart.

THIRTEEN

Devastator slammed into the shimmering energy field again, lashing out with his mighty strength in a futile attempt to break free.

Not for the first time, Skywarp said, "It's useless."

If Devastator can't break through it, Skywarp reasoned, then brute force wasn't going to get them out. There were few of their kind who were as strong as the massive Constructicon. He looked at the other Decepticons who had also been imprisoned by the Keepers after Starscream's death: Thundercracker, Buzzsaw, Laserbeak, Rumble and Shrapnel. There had been others in Las Vegas, too, but that had been late last night. Skywarp suspected that their cowardly natures had won out after Megatron and the others had left.

Perhaps they had joined him.

The others were now looking to him for leadership, which was only logical. He had allowed Starscream his little folly knowing that he could best him at any time…and certain that Megatron would be back. His time to lead the Decepticons would come eventually.

It had been, however, highly entertaining to watch Starscream's logic centers fall apart. A little gift from one extreme end of the electromagnetic spectrum that Skywarp had bestowed upon him. Now, though, it would be up to him to lead the remaining Decepticons and escape from this prison.

"Devastator!" he called to the being that was once again trying to bash his way through the barrier. "Enough!"

The titan turned to him with a look that said, in so many words, "Do *you* have a better idea?"

Skywarp did, indeed, have an idea. "Transform back into your individual modes," he said. "Brute force will not work against this barrier."

"Then what will?" Thundercracker harped.

Surprised that the cowardly bird had stayed around long enough to be captured, Skywarp said, "Nothing."

A jumble of complaining voices rose around him, and for a minute Skywarp felt a small sliver of pity for Megatron, who'd had to listen to this for so long. "Fighting the barrier makes it stronger," Skywarp explained. "Not fighting it will weaken it."

"So we're just supposed to sit here and do nothing?" Shrapnel asked. "What kind of plan is that?"

"I didn't say we would do nothing," he said. "Just nothing against the barrier."

He turned to the six Constructicons that comprised the awesome Devastator, now back in their original forms. He gestured at the dome-shaped barrier around them. "While this field surrounds us above, in front and behind, perhaps it *doesn't* do so everywhere."

Skywarp pointed at the desert floor beneath their feet and turned to Bonecrusher. "Feel like digging?" he asked.

The Keepers watched as one of them *became*

Starscream. His systems were modified, and an internal review of his mechanisms showed that an exceptionally strong electromagnetic pulse had damaged his logic center. This was repaired and altered to prevent it from happening again. Unlike the machine once called Bluestreak, Starscream's armor and primary components were far less damaged, so fewer mechanical alterations were required. His personality, the core essence of him, was contained much like Bluestreak's had been, in a mental prison that had no walls, no doors, no windows, and no way out.

The Keepers paused in the work to listen to his anguished howls as he tried and failed to break free. Eventually, he quieted.

The Voice shared an idea. *"Perhaps another demonstration of our power is necessary. The humans and the machines called Transformers continue to make plans against us."*

"To what end?" one Keeper wanted to know.

"These beings know what it is to fear. Why expend the energy defending ourselves when a simple demonstration might cow them into submission?"

"A valid point. What demonstration might we make?"

"One of the human prisoners who escaped our world is here—the one designated 'Melony'. Let us bring her here and transmit images of her being contained and altered by our powers. If we do it slowly enough, perhaps the humans will decide to be cooperative with their fate."

"Agreed."

The Keeper who had once been called Starscream rose to his feet, restored. *"I will retrieve her. The*

131

memory banks of this one tell me that those humans identified as law enforcers will cooperate with this form."

The other Keepers shared their agreement, and the new Starscream rose to his feet. Without another thought or word, he turned and headed for the Las Vegas jail. The Follower Melony, the one who was so angry and guilt-stricken, was about to be given a wonderful gift.

Melony heard the commotion outside, and sat up on the thin mattress on which she'd spent the night. The cell she was in—no interrogation room for the condemned to die—was dirty, and smelled of old urine. Which was understandable, given that the metal toilet was less than three feet away from the cot.

The night had been sleepless. Though she'd tried to rest, every time she closed her eyes images of her sister's death, her time on the Keepers' world, being *saved* by one of *them*, flashed before her eyes. When she realized that sleep was impossible, she lay awake and stared into the dark for a long time. She wondered what had happened to Paul, if he had made it to the Followers with Starscream's offer. He had been an interesting man, though his personal conflicts about God, and the Transformers, and saving others, were almost as alien to her as the Keepers.

She'd been unkind to him, but the minutes leading up to their departure from the Keepers' world had shaken her confidence badly. Melony hadn't realized that the potential to take another human life—as she'd tried to take Paul's—was in her. Her anger had always been directed at the Transformers. Stepping through the gate and into the chaos of her own world, seeing the battles being fought, people dying, buildings being crushed...she'd found it was a rerun of her sister's death.

Even when Paul had been hit with that tazer and they'd been taken into custody, she had continued to retreat within herself. It was only when Starscream had confronted her directly that she re-found her purpose, her voice, and her self. And now, that finding, the restoration of her personal balance, would be short-lived. Starscream had sentenced her to die.

At least then, she reflected, I won't have to face living.

The corridor echoed when the cellblock was opened, and a group of police officers, led by Captain Lomax, stopped outside her cell. Lomax obviously hadn't slept either. His dark eyes were puffy and red, his hair disheveled. He was wearing the same clothing he'd had on the night before.

"Is it time?" she asked him.

Lomax shook his head. "I don't know," he said. "I don't know what the hell is going on, and neither does anyone else."

"What do you mean?"

"Early this morning, one of the Keepers came and confronted Starscream...and killed him without barely lifting a finger. We all knew he was dead. Nothing could have survived the energy that creature poured into him." He gestured down the hallway and her cell opened.

She stood and crossed the short distance between them. "Starscream is dead?" she asked incredulously. Was she saved?

"We thought so," Lomax said. "The Keeper dragged him off. We've spent the whole morning trying to figure out what to do. The other Decepticons ran for it, but the Keepers imprisoned them outside the city."

"'Thought so'?" Melony asked, confused.

"He came back," Lomax said.

"What do you mean?"

"He's been…altered. Like Bluestreak. And now he's outside…asking for you."

"You mean he's a…he's a Keeper?" Melony gasped.

Lomax nodded. "Or worse," he said. "He sounds like Starscream, looks like Starscream mostly, but it *isn't* him."

Melony nodded. The Keepers wouldn't waste a being whose structure and form were so well suited to combat. They did enjoy their little spectacles. And, from all appearances, they didn't waste much of anything. She looked at Lomax and realized the man was scared witless. "Okay," she said, taking a deep breath. "Let's go."

"Melony," Lomax said, touching her on the shoulder. "I'm sorry."

She smiled at him. "I know," she said. "But you're just doing your job."

They walked down the long, lime-green-floored hallway, and somewhere Melony found the strength to hold her head up high. But inside, she could feel her show of bravery slowly unraveling, and her mind quietly beginning to jabber in pure, bona fide panic.

For now, though, she told herself, I can hang on.

I have to.

The former Starscream watched as Melony was led out of the jail. She held her head high, and kept her eyes locked straight ahead. When she stopped in front of him, he towered over her—a giant standing over an ant. The law enforcement officers milled around her, unsure of what to do next without a direct order.

The one called Lomax stepped forward. "As you commanded, Starscream," he said. His voice was shaking, and the Keeper could sense that a slight tremble was wracking his nervous system. Fear.

"Starscream is no more," the Keeper said. *"There are only the Keepers. We are your gods now."*

Lomax nodded, but didn't speak.

The Keeper knelt and picked Melony up in one hand, imprisoning her between the bars of his fingers. *"You are to be given a great gift,"* it said.

Obviously trying to be brave, she looked into the Keeper's eyes and said, "I want no gift from you, other than freedom."

"That option doesn't suit our needs," the Keeper said.

"And what is this gift?" Melony said.

"You will provide a lesson to all humanity," the Keeper said. *"Through you we shall demonstrate our power."*

"How's that?" she asked.

"You will become *one of us,"* it said. *"You shall be altered, your body and mind transformed into something more suitable for one of our kind."*

"Be...become?" she said. "A Keeper?"

"Yes," it said.

"I'd rather die!" she shouted.

"Have no fears on that account," the Keeper said to her, turning and heading back to where the others were gathered. *"You will."*

And that was when her courage broke. The Keeper laughed as she screamed in his iron fist. Peering into her mind, he could see her frantically trying to find a possible escape...and coming up so very, very empty.

Starscream had ceased trying to escape the prison of his own mind. Escape appeared to be impossible, and he forced himself to calm down. He reviewed everything that had happened since Megatron's disappearance and it was clear now, though it hadn't been then, that he wasn't functioning correctly. Why on Earth had he chosen Las Vegas to be his headquarters? It wasn't defensible in any practical sense, and the humans, while helpful with control of their own kind, brought little to the table that fear didn't accomplish on its own. Something had been done to him—and his taste for revenge was now growing rapidly.

But revenge was for another time.

Right now, he needed to focus his efforts on regaining control of his body and destroying the horrible being who had put him here. The prison was vast and dark, but if he must search every square centimeter of it he would.

He watched as Melony, the human he had sentenced to die, was brought out of the jail. The conversation with the Keeper, whose malevolence even he could feel, was horrifying to the human. Starscream understood the Keeper's point, however. If they altered her to become a Keeper, then the rest of the human race might face the same fate. It was possible, though unlikely in Starscream's estimation, that they might surrender, rather than risk becoming one of these alien beings themselves.

On the whole, Starscream admitted to himself, it was an interesting plan. They loved to show off their power, he realized. *Perhaps* that *is where I will find my answer. If I can see and hear everything that occurs with my body, perhaps the Keeper can see and hear everything I say.*

With that, Starscream began searching his prison, looking for nothing more complicated than a way to whisper in the Keeper's ear.

CHAPTER

FOURTEEN

As he finished outlining his thoughts on an alliance with Megatron and his Decepticon followers, Optimus Prime watched the expressions on the assembled Autobots' faces—they ranged from concern and consternation to anger and outrage. It wasn't exactly the response he was hoping for. Still, this was as good a group of soldiers as he could ask for.

In addition to Jazz, Bumblebee and Prowl, a handful of other Autobots had been chosen for this mission: Wheeljack, Ironhide, Ratchet and Sunstreaker. The others had been ordered to disperse to various places across the world in hopes that, if they failed—which seemed likely to Optimus—there would be other Autobots still left to continue the fight.

Ironhide spoke first. "You know I'm not much for talk, so I'll get right to it. Why in the world should we trust Megatron?"

Optimus smiled. Ironhide was one of his favorites. "We shouldn't," he said. "But in order to rid the Earth of the Keepers, we must set aside our distrust, always remembering that the Decepticons will stop at nothing to defeat us."

"So who's to say this *isn't* some sort of plot?"

Streetwise asked. "It wouldn't be the first time Megatron has tried to trick us."

"No, it wouldn't," Optimus admitted. "But I feel we have little choice. For *now*, the Keepers are much more a threat than the Decepticons."

"Optimus," Sunstreaker said, "if you say these Keepers are a bigger threat than the Decepticons, then I believe you. But I never thought I'd see the day when I'd be fighting *with* them, and not against them."

Sunstreaker was a solid fighter, Optimus thought, and he understood that his doubts—as well as the others—were well-placed. "I never thought I'd see it myself," he said. "But the fact remains: to defeat them, we need to work *with* Megatron, not against him."

The sound of running feet came from the hallway and Spike rushed in, with Franklin close behind. Optimus leapt up. "What is *he* doing here?"

Spike held up a hand. "Wait, Optimus. He came to warn us."

"About what?" Optimus said. "I warned you, Spike, that he is an augment and *not* to be trusted."

Franklin laughed. "You may be right about that," he said. "But we've got bigger worries than that right now."

"Such as?" Sunstreaker said, inching closer and obviously prepared to do battle if Prime gave the order.

"The military is going to launch a strike on Las Vegas," Franklin said. "A full-out assault."

"No!" Optimus shouted. "If they do that, thousands will die."

"I know," Franklin said. "So we've got to get in there before they do, and wipe these buggers out."

"That's easier said than done," Optimus said. "They

were able to hold Megatron and me easily. It was only with the help of the Matrix and Spike that we were able to defeat them and escape back to this world."

"I didn't do much," Spike mumbled. "At least that I know of."

"You did enough," Sunstreaker said. He patted Spike lightly on the shoulder. "You always have."

"How do you know this?" Optimus demanded of Franklin.

Franklin removed his identification from his pocket. "I work for the National Security Agency," he said. "I heard about the attack early this morning, been looking for you ever since."

"And how'd you find us?" Ironhide wanted to know.

"Easily enough," Franklin said. "I just looked for Spike."

"What do you mean?" Spike said.

Franklin pointed to Spike's coat pocket. "That little bauble you've got in there gives off a traceable signal—if you know what to look for."

Spike removed the crystal shard from his pocket to stare once more at the strange, pulsating markings on its bluish-white surface.

"It's an oddity," Franklin said. "But here's an interesting thought: if the crystal could summon the Keepers here, is there any reason to think it couldn't send them back?"

Megatron and the assembled Decepticons met with Optimus and the Autobots he'd chosen on the top of Hoover Dam in the mid-afternoon sunlight. A quick review of what everyone knew to date did little to inspire confidence. Fourteen against the combined might of the Keepers—who now included Starscream and Bluestreak in some type of altered form.

"So," Megatron said, "the humans are going to launch an assault."

Franklin, who'd come along more at Spike's insistence than anyone else's, nodded an affirmative.

"Excellent," Megatron said. "When is this supposed to take place?"

"My best sources tell me they plan to go just before sunrise tomorrow."

"Why is that excellent, Megatron?" Optimus asked.

"Because," Megatron replied, "while the Keepers are busy trying to eradicate the humans, we shall launch our own assault."

"We can't *use* them to cover ourselves," Optimus objected. "They'll be decimated!"

"That's what *soldiers* get paid for," Megatron hissed. "Do you have a better plan?"

Unfortunately, Optimus realized that he didn't have a better plan. "I dislike the thought of using human shields. They are not prepared for this kind of battle."

"*If* it's even a battle," Soundwave interjected. "From all Megatron has told me, and from what we've seen since they arrived here, they might just 'think' us all dead."

Megatron shook his head. "No, I don't think so."

"Why not?" Sunstreaker asked. "It's as easy as anything else."

"Because they *like* to demonstrate their power," Megatron reasoned, "if for no other purpose than their own amusement."

"They'll fight," Optimus agreed. He turned to

Franklin. "What if the assault fails?" he asked. "What will the military do?"

"For certain?" Franklin said. "I don't know. But I'd guess they'll launch a nuke and take out the whole city."

The Autobots chorused their disapproval. Even the Decepticons knew that this was an extreme answer.

"I didn't say I liked it," Franklin said, "but what other options do they have?"

"None," said Spike. "None whatsoever."

Optimus turned his attention back to Megatron. "Your plan, then, is to use the human assault as cover for our own. Go in on their coattails and attack at the same time."

"Not exactly," Megatron said. "Soundwave, play the newest transmission from Skywarp."

Soundwave stepped forward, and began to play the recording. "Megatron, if you're receiving this…we have found a way to breach the energy prison the Keepers have us in…. We went down instead of out…. I thought to have us escape, but have reconsidered…. What are your orders?"

Megatron laughed. "I told them to stay there. Before we attack the Keepers, our numbers will be even greater. We'll throw everything we have at them."

"Clever," Optimus acknowledged. "If the Keepers believe your forces are still imprisoned, they won't likely watch them as carefully."

"Indeed," Megatron said. "And with the human troops blasting away at them, they might not even notice they're gone until we're right on top of them."

"It's a sound plan, Megatron," Optimus said, "but I dislike the human casualties." He turned to the

Ratchet. "I'll want you to focus all your efforts on doing what you can to save human lives."

"But—" Megatron began to protest.

"No, Megatron," Optimus said. "I won't leave the humans to perish. You might be willing to do that, but I'm not."

Franklin suddenly shouted for quiet. "Are any of you able to pick up television broadcasts?"

The Keeper once known as Starscream ascended the hastily erected platform to join The Voice and the former Bluestreak. In front of the platform, Isolde Holden and her camera crew were preparing to broadcast live. Not that it mattered to the Keepers—they were perfectly capable of broadcasting their demonstration over every television in the country, which they fully intended to do.

The Voice stepped forward, and Isolde frantically waved her hands at her cameraman to start rolling. Across numerous channels and in numerous homes, the programming was suddenly overridden.

"People of the Earth," The Voice said. *"The being known as the Decepticon Starscream is no more. His so-called rule of Las Vegas has been terminated."* The Keeper gestured to the altered Starscream behind him.

"Even after we have shown you our power by destroying your city of Los Angeles, plots against us continue on. Therefore, as promised, we have chosen to give you another demonstration of our might." The Voice gestured, and a human woman was brought to the platform. She screeched and struggled, but was held tightly by several of the Keepers.

"What you are about to witness will be the fate of all if you fail to surrender," The Voice said.

One of the Keepers standing next to the woman, an almost gelatinous blob with sharp metal spikes protruding from it like some sort of ameba from Hell, lurched forward. As it enveloped her body, her screams were abruptly cut off.

Several more Keepers stepped forward, bearing a variety of mechanical devices. Some, like the large gears, were familiar to those watching. Others bore little or no resemblance to anything ever manufactured on this world. The Keepers worked quickly and, in a span of several minutes, the woman was altered horribly.

Her legs were now covered with metal trusses ending in metallic boots with knife-like blades protruding from the toe and heel. Her torso was coated with some kind of protective plating that gleamed in the afternoon sunlight. Her arms had, for all effective purposes, been removed and replaced with appendages whose sole purpose appeared to be the affliction of pain—her left arm was a whirling blade, her right, a laser weapon. Her head was helmeted, and radiating spikes shot out from where her once lustrous black hair had been. Only her face remained untouched. Perhaps leaving this tiny bit of beauty was the final blow.

The gelatinous Keeper was gone and in its place was this new *thing*.... A human transformed into a Keeper.

Isolde Holden could be heard wretching in the background, unable to broadcast a word.

One person watching the spectacle gritted his teeth in outrage. Paul Chateris silently vowed to avenge her death, though no one was aware of this silent promise—least of all the woman.

The Voice looked into the eyes of every watcher in the world. *"Surrender, or face this as your final destiny."*

The broadcast ceased.

Melony Harcourt felt her body stretching and changing as the Keepers altered it to suit their needs, yet there was no pain. Trapped within the same dark prison as Starscream and Bluestreak—though she didn't know it—for the first time in long years, she was...outside herself. Her retreat into the dark allowed her the luxury of being able to think past the immediate moments of her life and examine her choices with a greater perspective than ever before.

Her fears, she realized, had more to do with her own failings as a sister, even as a physician, than they did with how she felt about the Transformers.

Her guilt had become a scalpel upon which she cut her own soul; her hatred, an all-consuming passion that had left her a hollow shell of a complete person.

And Paul Chateris had seen right through it.

Though she knew she could look out through her own eyes, listen to the world with her own ears, even though she had no control over her body itself, Melony chose not to. Nor did she, much to the Keepers' surprise, search for a way to escape.

At present, she had no desire to do so. This newly-won balance within her was, she sensed, quite fragile. It was also immediately clear to her that escape would be difficult, if not impossible. She wanted time to explore her own feelings and actions and come to terms with them and herself.

She thought of her attempt to kill Paul by pushing him into the lava on the Keepers' world and felt grief, true grief, for the first time since she'd held her sister's dead body. She would, one day, very much like to apologize to him. He had shown amazing restraint and...compassion toward her, even after seeing what a heartless soul she had become.

And that's what she was now, Melony realized: a soul. A soul without a heaven, or even a hell. Adrift in her own mind, she was in a biological purgatory. The analogy would be pleasing to someone of Paul's educational background, she was certain. The Keepers called this transformation a gift, and perhaps in their minds it was. To most humans, it was horrific torture.

They were more right than they knew, she thought.

And then she realized something of dire importance, though there was no one she could tell. An idea that she immediately knew she must hide within herself.

Souls are bodiless.... They cannot be imprisoned. I can leave whenever I choose.

The only question is...where would I go?

FIFTEEN

T hree hours before sunrise, Paul was on the edge of Las Vegas, working his way down the Strip and feeling a little bit like he'd been assigned to a SWAT unit. Allister Greaves had been as good as his word, providing him with excellent tactical gear, maps of the city, and addresses for the last known locations of anyone in the Followers' organization. For the first time in long years, Paul felt like maybe he was doing something that mattered.

Seeing Melony so horribly altered had both angered and disgusted him. His self-control, something on which he prided himself, had nearly shattered. There could be no hope for her, he knew that now. But that didn't mean he couldn't keep his promise to himself: he would save her, just not in the way he'd hoped.

First, though, he had to get the others out. On the Strip itself, there was no need for anything other than moving quickly. The Decepticons were gone, Starscream was now a Keeper, and the local police appeared to have their hands full just trying to keep some semblance of order on the streets. He was just one more late night/early morning straggler, albeit one dressed in black body armor with a Ranger vest, a .9mm Glock with laser sights, and night vision goggles. In other parts of the world, he would stand out like a sore thumb. In the Las Vegas that now existed, he was just part of the scenery.

Stopping beneath the glow of the lights emanating from the Excalibur, Paul removed the city map from the cargo pocket on his pants and reviewed it along with the address list. His plan was to take them out of the city two at a time, using their own vehicles. He was just getting his bearings when he heard the noise.

The sound echoed over the city, and Paul placed it instantly: helicopters. He scanned the skyline. He couldn't see them yet, but there was plenty of glow from the lights to hide the sky from here. Perhaps it was a preliminary scouting run in advance of the military strike.

He listened again and waited, trying to distinguish how many there were.

A secondary sound joined the night air. Fighter jets overhead.

The military had moved sooner than expected, Paul realized. It wasn't a scouting mission.... It was an attack!

"They are coming," The Voice told the others.

"Yes."

"Do we stop them?"

Starscream laughed. *"Why? Let them come closer. Let them believe they can harm us. This body is almost enough to stop them by itself. When they reach us, we will punish them for their audacity."*

"How?"

Bluestreak also laughed. *"We will blow them from the sky."*

"Yes."

Starscream hated the sensation of being used. Under Megatron's chafing rule, he'd always felt less than appreciated for his contributions, but his old leader had never hesitated to order him into battle. The notion that this alien being was about to use him, but in a much more direct way, made Starscream livid, but he felt powerless to stop it.

There was no real way for him to take control of his body. He was bodiless, without form, and....

If I am without form, how can I be imprisoned?

If putting on the brakes were possible, Bluestreak would have done so. His confinement within the Keeper disgusted him. Should he ever be returned to himself, he knew that it would take years of washing before he felt clean again. Seeing what they'd done to that poor woman...and yet, there was nothing he could do.

He could not even deactivate himself. There was no shutting down the essence of himself, any more than he could capture a cloud in his fist. Visibly tangible, he'd often looked out on the sky and thought they looked solid enough to walk on. Had he tried it, he knew, he'd have found it differently.

Not everything was what it appeared to be. Bluestreak couldn't control himself, but he wasn't himself. He was...a cloud. A vapor. His form was determined by his thought. There was no physical body at all.

And if there's no physical body...*How can they keep me here?*

One of the devices Greaves had provided Paul with was a nifty earpiece module that allowed him to scan numerous radio and even sub-spectrum frequencies. As the first wave of choppers flew overhead, he rapidly flipped through them, and so it was that he was able to hear the communications of the attacking military:

"Eagle teams, we are one hundred and twenty seconds from the target. Report status. Eagle Team One."

"In formation. Cocked, locked, and ready to rock."

"Eagle Team Two."

"In formation."

"Eagle Team Three."

"In formation."

"Badger Team One."

"Scope is clear, we are set."

"Badger Team Two."

"In position."

Paul guessed that the Eagles were the three flights of choppers that had just passed overhead, while the Badgers must be ground troops.

"Hawkeye Team One, status."

"Full turn and circle set."

"Hawkeye Team Two."

"Full turn and circle set."

Those must be the jets, Paul thought. *They've gone past and scoped their targets and are on their way back.*

"All teams, the run is a go. Hawkeye, Eagle, Badger."

They're not particularly clever with their lingo, Paul thought. *Just about any damn fool could figure this out. And the Keepers are no fools.*

The jets were coming back. Paul could hear them, high up above the city, their engines screaming along right at the edge of the sound barrier. He was several long blocks from where the Keepers had stationed themselves, but that didn't prevent him from seeing Starscream blast up from the ground in a flare of jet engines more powerful than any human military plane.

Oh hell. They're going to get blown right out of the friggin' sky.

"Falcon, we have a bogey coming up at six o'clock."

"Confirmed, Hawkeye. We have a visual launch from within the city."

A moment of static, then, "Hawkeye teams, go to guns and evasive. It's Starscream."

"Roger, Falcon, we—"

Several streaks of fire lit the night, followed by a series of horrific explosions that lit up the clouds over the city like a surprise sunrise.

"Falcon, Hawkeye Team One is—No!"

The voice was cut off as another series of explosions blossomed overhead.

"Eagle Teams, move out!"

The choppers roared into the center of the city, and Paul watched as a blue beam of energy that resembled a bolt of lightning arched out of the area in front of the Seven Wonders Casino, lancing into the lead chopper. Crackling and snarling, the energy washed over the machine, which spun out of control and slammed into the ground.

A barrage of rockets was fired from the choppers, the ground around the casino exploding in a geyser of rock, dirt, and debris. The casino itself began to collapse. Automatic weapons fire ricocheted through the darkness, tracer rounds streaking through the night sky like bottle rockets.

"Falcon, there's some sort of…barrier around them."

"Keep firing, Eagle Teams. Badger Teams, move out!"

Four streaks of fire shot up from the ground, slamming into four of the helicopters with enough concussive force to shake the area. They exploded in balls of flame, burning pinwheels of radiant red and orange that fell from the sky.

The sudden shriek of jet engines burst overhead as the altered Starscream nosedived through the atmosphere. A flurry of cluster bombs arced out from his wings, bursting into the ground and leveling nearby buildings…along with the ground troops that had been moving up between them. Paul heard their agonized screams as many of them burned to death trying to escape the carnage.

They're all going to die, he realized. *And no one can stop it.*

When the first jets streaked overhead, Optimus' sensors told him they were military fighter planes. Not illogically, he at first assumed it was a preliminary scouting run before the planned pre-dawn assault. But when the helicopters thumped overhead, he knew that they'd changed plans.

"Megatron!" he called. "We've got to move out now!"

Megatron looked up from where he was sitting with his Decepticons. "What? Why?"

Optimus pointed at the sky. "They're launching the assault now! They're not waiting."

"We won't beat them there," Megatron said.

"Let's just get there," he yelled. "Autobots, roll out!"

"Decepticons! Move out!"

The group launched themselves at top speed toward Las Vegas.

The phone on Allister's desk rang, and his eyebrows arched in surprise. He rarely received calls at this hour. Picking up the phone, he said, "Greaves."

"Mr. Greaves," Elisa's voice said. "There's been a change of plans."

"How so?" he asked, fearing the worst.

He heard a brief, scuffling sound, and a stinging slap. Elisa cried out. A male voice came on the line.

"Mr. Greaves," the voice said.

"Who is this?" he demanded.

"Call me the party operator," the voice said. "The party you're trying to reach has been disconnected." A single, brief shot rang out.

"Elisa?" Allister asked. "Is she all right?"

"There will be a car coming to pick you up, Mr. Greaves. There's someone who'd very much like to speak with you. I suggest you take the ride."

The call disconnected.

Allister sighed. His contact, the Secretary to the President of the United States, had been found out. And so, it seemed, had he.

On one of the television screens, the driveway camera automatically zoomed in on the long, black car pulling up. It bore, he thought, some resemblance to a hearse.

The alliance of Autobots and Decepticons stopped outside the city limits. As soon as Skywarp and the others saw them, they exited their prison through a deep tunnel dug by Bonecrusher and excavated by Scavenger. The Keepers, it seemed to Optimus, took a lot for granted. A series of fireballs lit up the sky over the city, and Optimus yelled, "Hurry!"

The second they cleared the energy barrier, Skywarp looked at Optimus and Megatron standing side by side, and said, "It's only logical that we should combine forces."

"Of course it is, you fool!" Megatron said. He turned to the others. "Omega Sentinel, Devastator, transform and get going."

"Ratchet, get out there and do your thing," Optimus said. "Save as many as you can."

Franklin and Spike stepped out of Bumblebee. In his hand, Spike clutched the crystal shard. "Optimus, I need to get to the Keepers," he said. "I need to be close."

"You've remembered, then?" Optimus asked. "You know how to use it?"

Spike shook his head. "No, but maybe it will come to me. I just know I have to be close."

"Very well," Optimus said. "You'll come with me."

"As will I, if you don't mind," Franklin said. "I'll watch over him, while you're busy killing Keepers."

"I don't have time to argue the point," Optimus said. His instinct about Franklin said that he shouldn't trust him, he should keep Spike as far from him as possible, but…. Another round of explosions lit the night sky. This time from within the city itself. People were *dying* in there, and this might be their only chance to stop the Keepers.

"Get in," Optimus said, transforming into his giant red-and-white trailer mode. "Don't forget the plan," he said to Megatron.

"You can count on it," Megatron said. "Decepticons…" he pointed in the direction of the city, "attack and destroy the Keepers."

"Autobots," Optimus called out. "You have your orders, so let's get to it."

Optimus watched as Wheeljack, Thundercracker, and Laserbeak jetted into the sky, each heading for a different point on the compass. The savage Omega Sentinel began to circle to the north of the city—the direction his attack was supposed to come from, while Devastator headed south. Ratchet would follow him and Megatron into the heart of the city, and the battle, while the others scattered to various directions…each of them intent on reaching the Keepers at the same time.

As more explosions rocked the city, Optimus frowned. *If only the humans had trusted us with their plans…. We might have been able to save them.* He rolled into the outskirts of town, a city on the edge of complete annihilation.

CHAPTER

SIXTEEN

The Keeper who had identified himself as The Voice and the Keeper who had once been Melony shared their thoughts with each other.

They are coming, the Voice indicated.

Yes. All of them.

The others know this also.

It matters little whether they come or not. Like these humans, they shall be destroyed or altered to suit our needs.

The ones called Megatron and Optimus are different.

Yes. They shall have to be dealt with...harshly. To coin a most human phrase, if we give them an inch, they will take a mile.

Do they suspect about the source?

No. How could they?

Of course.

The Voice shared his process with the others. *Let them get close. We shall take them all at once.*

Yes.

Discarding stealth for speed, Paul ran as fast as he could manage through the screaming masses of people trying to get out of the city. Now that the battle was fully engaged, one end of the Strip was burning, and those who had been too stupid or too desperate to care finally pulled their heads away from their slot and keno machines to see the destruction headed their way. And then they ran like rabbits.

There was little point, Paul knew, in trying to get to the other Followers. And really, what point was there? Most likely, they had either fled or were in the midst of doing so even now. Several police vehicles screeched to a stop on the street, uniformed officers leaping out of their cars in an effort to control both the vehicle and pedestrian traffic. An effort, Paul guessed, that would be entirely futile.

Out of the corner of his eye, he saw Chief Lomax speaking into a shoulder mike, and trotted up to him. "Lomax!" he called.

"Chateris!" Lomax said, recognizing him. "What are you doing here?"

"I was going to try and help some people but it's probably too late for that."

"More Followers, like yourself?" Lomax asked.

"Yes, but how'd you..." Paul's voice trailed off as the realization struck him. "You're one of us, aren't you?"

Lomax nodded. "Yes," he said. "But it sure didn't turn out the way I expected."

Down the street, several of the choppers veered up and away, trying to escape Keeper Bluestreak's wrath. Shells exploded in the sky, and bolts of particle lighting arced and crackled. "It's falling apart here," Paul said. "Why didn't you help us?"

"I tried," Lomax said. "I did everything I could to convince Starscream you weren't worth questioning, but he's about three fuses short of a circuit. Or he was." He jammed a thumb in the direction of the Seven Wonders Casino. "Now, he's just one of them."

"What about Melony?" Paul asked.

"She's with them," Lomax said. "She's *one of them.*"

"I know," Paul said. "But I promised myself I'd save her."

"How?" Lomax demanded. "Those creatures make Transformers look like kiddy toys."

For a moment, Paul was silent. "I have to kill her," he finally said. "It's all I can do."

Lomax shook his head. "I think about all you'll manage is to get yourself killed."

Paul chuckled. "After the last few days, my own skin is the one thing I'm not all that concerned about."

A woman ran screaming past them, an infant child wrapped in a blanket that trailed behind her clasped in her arms. Not realizing that the blanket was on fire and that running was making it worse, the woman went past them without a glance. Paul started to reach for her, but one of the uniformed officers stepped in front of her, wrapped her in his arms, while another stomped on the blanket.

Lomax turned his attention back to Paul. "Most of the other Followers are either gone or missing," he said. "I got a message to try and get them clear. The ones I was able to find are already on the outskirts of the city or past it."

"Good," Paul said. "At least they'll make it."

The sound of a LAW rocket slamming into a building, followed by automatic gunfire momentarily stopped their conversation. "Unless this spreads out," Lomax said. "I've got to go. Got a city to try and protect."

"Yeah," Paul said. "And I've got a soul to save." He offered his hand, and Lomax shook. "Good luck to you," Paul added.

"You, too," Lomax said.

As Paul turned to head back down the street, Lomax called out to him. "Hey Paul?"

"Yes?"

"Who's soul are you going to save? Hers or yours?"

Paul thought for a moment and shrugged. "I don't think it really matters," he said, then turned and headed towards the front lines.

As he ran, he turned back on the earpiece in time to hear another brief spatter of communications by the military that sent a chill up his spine.

"All teams, all teams, this is Falcon. Fall back to rendezvous point Delta. Visual confirmation of all parties is achieved. The weapon is hot. I say again, the weapon is hot."

Omega Sentinel stalked down Quill Gordon Avenue, a small suburban road on the north side of Las Vegas, ignoring both humans and their habitations. He was hunting, and while Megatron had ordered him to close on the Keepers from this direction, what he really wanted to do was find Starscream and destroy him. Twice, now, the altered Decepticon had flown past him at long range, using his weapons to lay waste to the military ground troops below.

Starscream had failed—both as a Decepticon and as a leader—and every one of his logic circuits dictated that the penalty for these failures should be death. It was the way of the Decepticons.

A jet screamed overhead, and in one fluid movement, Omega Sentinel spun, tracking the object in milliseconds. His gigantic left foot came down on a garage. The jet was a military plane, so he ignored it, turning instead to resume his steady advance into the heart of Las Vegas.

At his feet, his sensors noted a shrill-voiced female human. As a rule, Omega Sentinel ignored humans altogether—they were neither logical nor of any particular use to him—the way a giant would ignore an ant, but her piercing voice got his attention. That, and the fact that humans usually ran *from* him, not toward him.

"Hey you! Don't you know I'm *working* here?" She shook a finger at him, as though he were an errant three-year old. "Take your battle someplace else."

At the woman's feet a swarm of mewling cats tried to trip her up. She was wearing a fuzzy pink bathrobe and her dark blonde hair stood out in all directions as though it had not seen the right side of a brush in several days. Completely and utterly confounded by her verbal assault, Omega Sentinel stared down at her.

"I'm under *deadline*," the woman said. "I've got an editor who harangues me every day, and no excuses about rampaging aliens or Decepticons is going to get me a minute longer and—" She broke off her tirade to shoo a cat out of the way. "And then you come along and crush my garage! Shoo! Scat!"

The woman was making wild gestures with her arms. "Do you know how close you came to destroying my *office*?"

With a snarl of outrage, Omega Sentinel decided that this nuisance had to be stopped. Her screeching voice alone was enough to overload his sensors, and she was distracting. He slammed a fist into the woman's house, shattering it like kindling.

Now the woman really did begin screaming, though it was unclear which upset her the most. "My house! My cats! My book!" She went tearing into the rubble, bathrobe flailing, as she searched for whichever item seemed most valuable.

With a disgruntled shrug and the internal knowledge that he would *never* understand humans, let alone human females, he continued on into the city. His sensors sweeping the night sky for any sign of Starscream.

Devastator smashed through the south end of the city like a giant wrecking ball. Slow, to be sure, but his advance was steady. For once, all six of his components were in agreement about a course of action. Destroy the Keepers...and anything that got in his way.

Two blocks over, a flight of retreating Apache helicopters flew past, heading south. Devastator ignored them much as he did the fleeing humans on the street. Cars, buses, motorcycles and even the occasional person dumb enough to cross into his path were crushed under his feet.

He was getting fairly close to his target now, as the explosions and gunfire were less than a block away. Suddenly, he caught a glimpse of Bluestreak. His understanding of what the Keepers were, what they had done, was limited. But he was clear on one thing: this was an Autobot he *could* destroy. Megatron had said that Bluestreak wasn't himself at all, but a Keeper who had taken him over.

With a terrifying howl, he turned in the direction

the being had taken, and began to power up his solar energy rifle. One burst from that at 10,000 degrees centigrade would most certainly wipe the alien right off the planet.

"Come, Bluestreak," he called. "Come and fight Devastator!"

Weaving in and out of the wreckage of cars, the debris of collapsed buildings, and fleeing pedestrians took all of Optimus Primes' skill. Strapped in to the front seat, Spike and Franklin called out the occasional warning, but were otherwise silent.

Megatron was close behind, and Optimus called out to him. "We're almost on top of them!"

Overhead, Wheeljack, Thundercracker and Laserbeak began their straffing runs. Not even the altered Starscream could engage all three at once, though the sky was nearly as bright as day as rockets and other weapons were activated.

"Spike, as soon as I stop, you've got to jump out and find a good hiding place," Optimus called.

A rocket fired from a nearby alley streaked past the windshield, and Spike said, "No argument here."

Prime locked his brakes up half a block from the Seven Wonders Casino, and Spike and Franklin jumped out. Behind them, Megatron stopped and transformed into his weapon mode, while Optimus shifted back into his normal, robot form.

He picked up Megatron in one hand, and turned to Spike and Franklin. "Get out of here, both of you," he said. "And be safe."

"You, too, Optimus," Spike said, as Franklin grabbed him by the arm and began pulling him away.

"Ready?" Optimus asked Megatron.

"*I* am *always* ready," Megatron said.

Accessing the energy from the Matrix, Prime began dodging forward. *This time*, he vowed silently, *I will finish what I started.*

Allister stepped out his front door and calmly walked down the steps to the front drive. The back door closest to him on the limo opened and he eased himself inside. It was dark, but his eyes adjusted quickly. There were three forms seated in the back, one of whom tapped rapidly on the glass. The driver engaged the transmission, and sped out of Allister's estate.

"Mr. Greaves," a familiar voice said. "When we tracked you down, I must admit to my own surprise. I'd heard you were dead."

Trying to place the voice, Allister chuckled. "I get that a lot these days."

"I suppose you do at that," the voice said. "Do you know why I'm here?"

Allister considered trying to play coy, but discarded the idea. If these people had wanted him dead, he would be. "I assume because you've figured out that I lead the organization known as the Followers," he said. "Also because you've figured out that I have ears in many places. High places."

"Indeed you do, Mr. Greaves. Of course, we allowed those exchanges to take place because it gave us time to track you. You obviously weren't selling the information you were getting," the voice said.

It was a deep voice, with a slight rasp to it. The tones were cultured. The cadence of speech measured.

"No," Allister said. "I have no need for money. I used the information for myself."

"Yes, you have," the voice responded. "Nonetheless, there are penalties for spying."

That was when it hit him. He knew who the voice was, and it shocked him deeply. "I would think," he said carefully, "that rather than assess penalties, we should discuss what we can do for each other." He leaned forward, his soft smile barely visible in the dark. Allister had guessed they'd sent a lackey, and they had, but a highly placed lackey regardless.

"Don't you, Mr. Vice President?"

They are many, the Keepers thought to each other.

Yes. But when they are close enough...

These forms limit us physically, but our will is strong. Our enemies do not know this.

The Keeper called The Voice shared his thought. *The problem is one of mobility. We cannot stay here; we cannot go elsewhere.*

Then we must destroy them, before they destroy us.

Yes. How?

The Keeper called The Voice was about to offer a solution when a new sensation entered his body. A tremor shook him from his metal-bladed head to his feet. The Voice had no name for this sensation.

The others called to him. *What troubles you?*

I do not know, The Voice thought. *I...*

Yes?

The Voice tried to rise, to stand, to shake off the tremors racking his body, but his joints refused to respond.

What is wrong? the others cried. The emotions churning from the one called The Voice frightened them.

I cannot move.

Why?

Something has me, The Voice noted. *Something is in me.*

What?

Me, Melony thought to them. *And now all of you are mine!*

SEVENTEEN

Huddled near the base of the large platform erected by the Keepers for their broadcast demonstration, Spike and Franklin paused to catch their breath. Or rather, Spike realized, paused to let him catch his breath. The NSA Agent hadn't even broken a sweat, let alone lost his breath.

"Now....what?" Spike puffed.

"You're the man with the memory problems," Franklin said. "Not me." He lifted his hands. "I'm just here to try and keep you alive long enough to open that gate and send them back to whatever hell they came out of."

Spike withdrew the crystal from his coat pocket and stared at it for a long minute. "I wish I knew how."

A pulsing arc of electricity shot out of a nearby alley, burst through a concrete wall and slammed into several soldiers who were trying to make a hasty retreat. In the distance, Spike could hear the grinding roar of Devastator calling out for Bluestreak to come and do battle with him. Strangely, Spike felt no real fear, but rather a sense of....elation. As if some part of him remembered being a Transformer, the call of battle, and could still enjoy it.

He stared out at the street, at the pedestrians who ran screaming in all directions, and saw something that rather surprised him. One man, dressed like a member of an elite S.W.A.T. team, was headed *this* way, instead of running in the other direction. He was good looking, in a male underwear model kind of way, but the set of his face—easily visible with the flares lighting up the night sky—was gravely serious. This was a man on a mission who would let very little stand in his way.

Intrigued, Spike raised a hand and whistled as loudly as he could. Beside him, Franklin nearly choked on his tongue and yanked Spike's arm down. "What the hell are you doing?" he hissed. "Trying to attract attention?"

"Look at that guy," Spike said, pointing him out. "All the police and soldiers are fleeing the area, but this one isn't. I want to know why." He shrugged. "Maybe he knows something we don't know."

The man saw Spike and Franklin near the platform and made his way in a zig-zagging pattern across the open expanse of lawn—most of which was cratered by shells. When he neared them, he ducked down next to them.

"Don't I know you?" he asked Spike.

"Maybe," Spike said, introducing himself.

"Oh yeah," he said. "You're buddy-buddy with the Autobots."

Spike nodded. "They are my friends, yes."

"Paul Chateris," the man said, by way of introduction. "Good to meet you."

They shook, and Spike began to tell him who Franklin was, when Paul interrupted him. "We already know each other, don't we...John?"

Spike looked at Franklin. "John?" he asked quizzically.

"Just a random name," Franklin said. "I suppose you may as well know. I'm Franklin Townsend."

"You're a lot of things, aren't you?" Paul asked.

"I'm diverse," Franklin said.

"That's one way to put it." Paul turned back to Spike. "What are you doing here in the middle of a war zone?"

Spike showed Paul the crystal. "This is what opened the gate for the Keepers to come to our world. I'm hoping it will send them back."

"You know how to use that thing?"

"Not really," Spike said. "But maybe something will come to me."

Paul laughed. "It might."

Suddenly, Franklin held up his hands for quiet and clapped one hand against his ear, as though trying to drown out the noise. "Shhh!" he hissed. He listened for a moment, and then his face went completely ashen. "Oh holy Mary, mother of God," he said.

He turned to Spike and Paul. "We've got to get out of here," he said. "We've got to get out of here *right now*."

Now that he'd correctly identified his visitor, Allister relaxed. One of the nice things about having a large information network was the ability to *have* information. And information about the vice president, he had in spades. The man had more skeletons in his closet than a serial killer, and Allister knew about a great many of them. Thanks, in no small part, to the now deceased Elisa.

"So you know who I am," the vice president said.

"Not a big deal, really. The point of this visit has to do with two things. First, your spying activities, including putting one of our NSA field agents on your payroll. Second, your organization, which now, according to our most recent figures, has at least one active member in every major city in the world—many of them highly placed."

Allister feigned boredom. In truth, he was fascinated. "You mean Agent Townsend? He's been a marvelous help, really."

"He's about to be put out to pasture," the Vice President said. "Along with a great many other people."

"A shame," Allister said. "He's quite good at his job."

"Which one?" he snapped. "Yours or ours?"

"Both, as far as I'm aware," Allister said. "Unless there's been some complaint about his performance on your end of things?"

"Funny, Mr. Greaves. I see you have a sense of humor."

"At my age, a sense of humor is a prerequisite to happiness."

"As for your organization…"

Allister held up his hand. "Last time I checked, having a private organization was still legal in the United States."

"Oh, it is," the vice president assured him. "Unless it's a cover for other activities, like spying."

"We are purely interested in learning about the Transformers," Allister said blithely. "Our interests stop there."

"Then why was Elisa on your payroll? Why is

Agent Townsend, even as we speak, doing work for you *inside* Las Vegas?"

"An errand, really," Allister said. "I have some people in there I wanted to get out safely. That city has become quite dangerous hasn't it?"

"You've no idea," the vice president said coldly. "You know about the military attack?"

Allister nodded, wondering where the man was going now.

"Why don't we see how things are going?" he suggested. He turned to one of his silent companions, a large brute of a man that was, no doubt, part of the Secret Service. The agent pushed a button and a small television popped up from a center console. He turned it on, and the picture, transmitted via satellite, appeared.

It was a small briefing room. Inside, the president, the chairman of the Joint Chiefs of Staff, and no small number of generals watched a heads-up display with interest.

"Mr. President," the vice president said. "We're *all* here, watching as we speak."

The president turned to face the camera. "Ahh, Mr. Greaves. How good of you to join us this morning."

"Mr. President," Allister said.

"I thought you might be interested in what's happening here," the president continued, "since your informant is rather....indisposed."

"You are correct, sir," Allister said. "I *am* interested."

"Good," the president replied. "Enjoy the show." He turned back to conferring with the people seated at the table. Their conversation was muted, but intense. One of them flicked a switch, and Allister could hear a live audio feed:

"*All teams, all teams, this is Falcon. Fall back to rendezvous point Delta. Visual confirmation of all parties is achieved. The weapon is hot. I say again, the weapon is hot.*"

Allister shuddered. *My God! They're going to launch a nuke!*

The president turned back to the camera. "You see, Mr. Greaves, I'm going to solve several of our nations problems at once. First, I'm going to dispose of those nasty aliens who call themselves the Keepers. Second, I'm going to eradicate the Transformers—Autobots and Decepticons alike. And third, after we've gathered up all the pieces—many of which, my scientists inform me, will survive even a nuclear blast—I'm going to use you and your Followers to rebuild them…under the federal government's direct supervision." He laughed softly. "That's why you're here this morning, Mr. Greaves. I'm giving you your wish…you're going to get to know all about the Transformers. From the inside out."

Allister felt the blood drain from his face. A nuclear weapon dropped into the middle of Las Vegas. The President could blame the Autobots and Decepticons for it, and no one would suspect a thing after the Los Angeles incident. Thousands, perhaps millions of people, would die. He'd never intended this, never wanted this. He was a man of science, of invention, and the Transformers had represented to him the possibility of new achievements never before imagined. But to have so many die….

He turned to the vice president. "Would it be all right if I made a phone call?"

The vice president laughed. "Certainly. There's nothing you can do to stop this after all."

Allister removed a small phone from his suit jacket pocket and dialed a number. On the screen, the President was giving the authorization codes for a launch. He glanced once back at the camera, turned back to the assembled staff and said, "Operation Phoenix Ashes is a go. Full authorization is given. Launch the warhead."

The phone answered on the third ring, and Allister spoke rapidly but clearly, knowing in his heart that it would never be enough.

"What?" Spike asked as Franklin jumped to his feet. "What the hell are you talking about?"

Exasperated, Franklin yanked out his earpiece and shoved it in Paul's ear. "Listen!" he said.

"Franklin and Chateris, this is Greaves. A nuclear launch has been authorized and ordered. It's a trap—for all of you. Warn the Autobots and get out, man! Get out while you can!"

Spike felt his jaw drop open, saw the look on Paul's face as he, too, heard the message in his own ear. Without another word, he turned and sprinted towards where Optimus and Megatron had just engaged the Keepers.

How long have we got? Paul wondered as he ran.

The answer occurred to him, and a moment of almost unreasoning fear nearly made him stop and run for his life.

Not very long at all.

The Keeper who had once been called Bluestreak saw the towering Decepticon that called itself Devastator. It wanted to fight. Which the Keeper found vastly amusing. The size of the machine mattered little. This body was incredibly fast and well-made, the enhancements that had been added by the Keepers would protect it from almost anything.

"Come, Bluestreak!" it called. "Come fight Devastator!"

The Keeper whipped itself around a corner. The machine was not fast nor particularly graceful, he saw, as it stepped on cars, jostled buildings, and tramped through the streets like a giant wrecking ball. Around another corner and behind it.

The Keeper aimed at the Decepticon's back and fired his ion-charged disperser rifle. This weapon, which had proved so effective against the helicopters earlier, electrified the particles in the air and presented itself as a bolt of lightning that slammed into Devastator's back with 80,000 volts worth of energy. A snarling crackle sounded as the bolt penetrated the armor of the titan.

Devastator turned awkwardly, roaring in outrage. His feet came down so hard that the ground shook, and the Keeper stumbled slightly trying to keep his balance. Not one for subtlety, Devastator pulled up his own solar energy rifle and fired.

A beam of intense heat slammed into the Keeper's body and for the first time, he felt something akin to pain as he danced backward trying to escape it. The armor of the creature once known as Bluestreak was not impervious to everything, and the Keeper knew that on this planet, their bodies were susceptible to damage, even if their minds were not.

Using his advantage of speed, the Keeper raced between Devastator's legs and whipped around a corner. Better, he decided, to be among his brethren to fight this creature. Their combined powers would be more than capable of stopping it.

Behind him, he sensed that Devastator had turned and was continuing his slow pursuit. In a way, the Decepticon was mindless—living only to destroy its targets. That, thought the Keeper, was almost frightening.

For without a mind, what can we do against it?

The Keeper who had once been known as the Decepticon Starscream saw the black and gold monstrosity identified as Omega Sentinel stalking towards the Las Vegas Strip with the single-minded glare of a hunting cat. *Now this*, the Keeper decided, *was an enemy worthy of his efforts.*

Beginning a steep nosedive towards his target, the Keeper targeted Omega Sentinel with his null-ray, intent on disabling the monster before blowing it into fragments. As he fired, however, the gigantic robot spun with the grace of a ballet dancer, and the ray bounced harmless off some sort of electric field.

Omega Sentinel immediately fired his laser cannon and the explosive force of the impact almost knocked the Keeper out of the sky. He noted that his own gyrocircuits were overloaded, and felt vaguely disoriented.

"Starscream!" Omega Sentinel called. "I see you!"

The Keeper tried to pull out of the dive before slamming into the ground, and just managed it. As he began to lift away from the ground, Omega Sentinel fired again, this time launching several mortar rounds from hidden bays in his feet.

Knowing that this form limited him, that his mind was stronger with his brethren present, the Keeper hit the jets and thrust himself back towards where the others were.

Behind him, he heard Omega Sentinel continue his advance, calling out, "You can run, failure, but you cannot hide."

This one, the Keeper realized, *was a nearly perfect killing machine. It would require a substantial effort to destroy it*. As he landed near the other Keepers, he realized something else.

There would be no help forthcoming from the others.

Something had gone horribly wrong.

EIGHTEEN

The Black Hills of South Dakota are vast expanses of rock and prairie grasses, rolling waves of dirt that can seem to go on for miles and miles in every direction. These lands are where the great herds of buffalo ran with the Sioux many years ago. Now, the land is dedicated to reservations, ranches, and...the federal government.

In a small underground bunker about the size of a double-wide trailer, well-shielded by nearby hills, and almost invisible unless one were standing right on top of it, two officers in a secure control room heard their orders from the president of the United States of America.

A long, quiet stare passed between the two, though neither one spoke. Finally, the senior man, a major by the name of William Backes, keyed a small safe and opened the daily codebook.

He reached for the transmitter, which broadcast on a very carefully screened and satellite bounced frequency, and said, "Condor, Condor, please repeat and confirm your transmission."

The voice came back again. "Alpha Base, this is Condor. I say again, this is Condor. Transmission confirmed. Red launch is ordered. Target coordinates—longitude 36.1695 degrees, latitude negative 115.2602 degrees."

The other officer, a younger woman who'd only made captain two weeks ago, rapidly keyed in the target coordinates, and with a startled intake of breath said, "Las Vegas."

Condor continued his transmission. "Authorization code is: Delta-Alpha-Victor-India-Sierra, Romeo-Uniform-Sierra-Sierra-Echo-Lima-Lima."

Major Backes looked between his notes and his codebook for a minute, then replied quietly, "Transmission confirmed, Condor. Red launch is ordered. Target coordinates—longitude 36.1695 degrees, latitude negative 115.2602 degrees. Authorization code is: Delta-Alpha-Victor-India-Sierra; Romeo-Uniform-Sierra-Sierra-Echo-Lima-Lima. Confirm?"

"Transmission confirmed, Alpha Base. Do right by us, boys. This is Condor, out."

The broadcast immediately ceased.

The young captain, whose last name was Wolfe, said softly, "Were we just ordered to launch a warhead at Las Vegas, sir?"

The major sighed. The benefits of being an officer in the middle of nowhere had quickly been overshadowed by the reality of a job he never thought he'd have to do. "Yes, Captain. Those were the orders, and the codes confirmed it."

"Shouldn't we—?"

"No, we shouldn't," the Major said. "If we think about it too much, we'll never do it."

"Yes, sir," Captain Wolfe said. "But we're talking about Americans, sir. One phone call."

"Captain, that's enough!" the major said. "We've gotten the order, with confirmed codes twice."

"Yes, sir."

Major Backes sat down and removed two keys from the safe. He handed one to Captain Wolfe, who was flipping several toggle switches. Overhead, they could hear the sound of the bay doors opening.

"Ready?" Major Backes asked her.

"Yes, sir," she said.

They both held their keys in front of circular slots on the console in front of them, looked briefly at each other and inserted them at the same time.

A computerized voice said, "Launch system keyed."

"First turn," Major Backes said. "Ready, set, now."

They turned their keys one click to the right.

The computer voice said, "Launch sequence initiated."

"Second turn. Ready, set, now."

Another click to the right.

"Launch countdown pre-initiated."

"Last turn. Ready, set, now."

Another click, back to the left.

"Launch countdown started. Launch in t-minus three minutes and counting."

"Did we do the right thing, sir?" Captain Wolfe asked him.

The Major turned and looked at her, ignoring the sparkle of tears in her eyes and striving not to shed his own. "I don't know, Captain. I just don't know."

In the bay, the growing thrust of the propulsion system used by the short-range nuclear warhead fired, filling the bay with smoke. The computer voice continued to count down, now at two minutes, forty-eight seconds.

When it hit, it would do enough damage to take out every living soul in the city of Las Vegas…the city of the damned and the desperate.

NINETEEN

Optimus was confused. Surely by now, the Keepers would have seen him. He'd made no effort to hide himself. But instead, they stood in a semi-circle, mouths agape as though so thoroughly surprised they'd forgotten to control their own bodies. He sighted in on the first one, while Megatron hissed, "Shoot them! Shoot them, now!"

As his finger tightened on the trigger, one of the Keepers—the one that had called itself The Voice, suddenly lashed out at the others with a cruel, bladed handed that moved like lightning. It took the first one directly in the chest, the blade buried deeply inside the metal casing protecting the hapless Keepers chest. It screamed and gibbered as The Voice raised it up overhead and tossed it aside like garbage.

"They're fighting amongst themselves," Megatron said. "Shoot them now!"

Optimus opened fire, pulling the trigger of the weapon Megatron had become and arcing a deadly red fire across the lawn.

Two Keepers landed on the lawn, both of them more

than familiar to Bumblebee. The first to skid to a stop in the grass had once been his good friend Bluestreak. The second had once been his enemy, the hated Starscream. At least one thing hadn't changed, Bumblebee reflected.

"Do you see them, Prowl?" he asked.

"Oh yeah," he said, "and this time I'm going to—what?"

Bumblebee turned back to the lawn in time to see both Soundwave and Skywarp slam into the two Keepers, the latter of which, at thirty-five-feet tall, hit Bluestreak full force, driving him backwards into the turf.

"Surprise," he said coldly, and cut loose with his primary weapon: a ray gun that emitted a coruscating beam of energy. Explosive gamma-radiation slammed into the Keeper, who emitted a howl of outrage and pain.

Soundwave, too, opened fire on the surprised Keeper who had altered Starscream. A burst of sonic-waves, amplified by a small dish on his arm, pounded the air so forcefully that the Keeper was literally driven backwards to smash into and then over a parked car that had somehow avoided any damage prior to that moment.

The two Keepers, however, were more than ready to fight. "We must—" the first Keeper said. "Join," said the second, completing the sentence.

The two of them raced toward each other, the forms of Bluestreak and Starscream altering as they ran, their armor running like liquid metal and reshaping itself. At full-speed they collided with one another.

The sight was so unlike anything Soundwave or Skywarp had ever seen that both of them stood there, momentarily stunned by the sight of a Decepticon and an Autobot...becoming one machine.

"That can't be good," said Bumblebee from where he and Prowl were observing the battle.

"I don't think so either," Prowl rumbled. He scanned the streets. "This is about to get *very* messy. Look." He pointed. From one direction, the massive Devastator approached, roaring Bluestreak's name. From the other, the monstrous warrior Omega Sentinel moved smoothly down the crowded street.

Several blocks down, Ratchet was doing his level best to herd panicked humans away from the main battle area. Most of the soldiers had either fled or been killed in the earlier fighting, though several diehards had remained behind. Launching the occasional rocket or using automatic weapons to fire on the Keepers whenever a shot appeared. For the most part, these attacks seemed useless to Bumblebee.

The Keepers had created some kind of protective field around the platform on which they were huddled. The rockets and bullets—at least those of human manufacture—bounced off the shield to slam into buildings, cars, and once every so often, a person dodging between the buildings.

"Look at that," Prowl said, pointing again.

Running across the lawn were three humans, two of which Bumblebee recognized immediately. The first was Spike, the second his friend, Franklin. The third Bumblebee did not know. What he did know was that they were all running towards where Optimus, using Megatron as a weapon, were just now opening fire on the Keepers.

And all three were in horrific danger.

Bumblebee threw himself across the yard in a full

sprint, calling Spike's name. Behind him, he heard Prowl call out for him to get down. "Spike!" Bumblebee yelled. "Get out of there!"

Spike slid to a stop, turned and saw Bumblebee racing across the lawn, Prowl several strides back.

Both Franklin and Paul slammed into the suddenly immobile Spike, knocking him to the ground, a fact for which Bumblebee was profoundly grateful when one of the shots fired by Optimus slammed into the Keepers' shield and rebounded directly over their heads.

Reaching Spike, Bumblebee knelt down and yelled, "What the slag are you doing?" Spike's face was ashen, he saw, but spots of high color flared on his cheeks.

"It's a trap," he gasped. "They're launching a nuke!"

Prowl arrived just in time to hear this revelation, but rather than stop, he kept right on running, obviously intent on getting to Optimus with this information.

"Oh no," Bumblebee said.

"Yes," Spike said. "So let's get the hell out of here, while we still can."

Bumblebee looked down the street where thousands of people were still trying to flee the city. "All those people..."

"And us, too, if we don't get out of here right now," Franklin said.

"I don't think we can," Paul said, pointing to the edge of the lawn.

"Why the hell not?" Franklin snarled before he looked and saw what Paul was pointing at.

Bumblebee and Spike both looked up at the same time. Across the street, a shimmering field of energy, much like the one protecting the Keepers had appeared. On the outside, Devastator and Omega Sentinel were both smashing at it with everything they had...to no effect.

The new form of the combined Starscream and Bluestreak snarled down at Skywarp and Soundwave. "You pitiful fools! Now you will both pay the price for your audacity!"

Controlling the body of the Keeper who had called itself The Voice wasn't easy. It resisted every mental demand Melony made of it. She was also certain that she would be unable to sustain her control over it for very long. Unlike the Keepers, who had apparently had millennia of practice using their minds as a weapon, Melony was unfamiliar with this. Soon enough, he'll fight through and get control back and I'll either be dead on right back in my mental prison cell, she thought.

As she struck out at the nearest of the others, intent on ripping as many of them into pieces as possible, she did realize that she had one advantage—a fact very clear in the Keepers scampering thoughts: no race the Keepers had ever encountered before had been able to do this to them. She slashed out with the metal bladed arm of the Keeper, driving it deep into the chest of one of the others.

Certainly, she was surprised by their delayed reactions. She had thought they would be on her in seconds, but instead they were milling around in confusion. All of the Keepers on the platform were being protected by some kind of energy barrier. Looking out through the creature's eyes, she could see that even the mighty Optimus Prime's weapon was unable to penetrate it.

She continued moving, slashing and gouging. Melony knew she wasn't doing much real damage.... That would be, she supposed, nearly impossible. From all appearances, the Keepers appeared to be nearly immune to physical harm. She was, she noticed, doing a good job at creating lots of chaos.

The idea of one of their own attacking them was obviously problematic for them.

She reached out for another one of the aliens, intent on severing its oddly-shaped head from the rest of its mechanical body, doing her level best to ignore the gibbering, pleading mental voice of the Keeper she had inhabited.

Even when it promised to restore her to her own body, to repair everything that had been done to her, Melony kept on.... These creatures were far worse, and far easier to hate, than any Transformer she'd ever seen.

"Optimus!" Prowl yelled. "Optimus, it's no good!"

"What are you talking about?" Optimus said, turning from his deliberate attempt to break through the shield the Keepers had erected.

"This whole set-up is some kind of trap," Prowl said. "The military has launched a nuclear warhead."

"*Why?*" Prime asked, hearing the pleading sound in his own voice and hating it. "Why would they do such a thing to their own people?"

"I don't know," Prowl said. "We can figure that out *later*, after we get out of here."

Prime glanced at the Keepers on the platform, one of whom was cutting through the others like a scythe through wheat, albeit a fairly uncoordinated scythe. "Well, we're certainly not blasting through that barrier they've erected." He set down the transformed Megatron. "We're going to have to try something else."

Megatron transformed back into robot form with a snarl. "This whole thing has gone to slag," he said. "Look."

Optimus and Prowl looked across the cratered lawn where he pointed to see the melded Starscream/Bluestreak/Keeper confronting Soundwave and Skywarp. On the far side of them, another energy barrier had been erected, locking out Devastator and Omega Sentinel, who were mindless killing machines....without anything to kill.

Scanning the area, Optimus said, "Who are we missing?"

"Looks like Wheeljack, Thundercracker and Laser-beak," Prowl said. "And Ratchet is still trying to get all those humans out of the area."

"All right," Optimus said. "First things first. If we can't get at the Keepers on the platform, and we can't get out, let's eliminate the immediate threat of that...thing."

Megatron nodded agreement, even as Skywarp fired his machine guns, blasting at it for all he was worth.

"Maybe if we all jump it at once...." Prowl suggested, as the three of them ran to join the battle.

Under normal circumstances, if Bluestreak had run into a Decepticon—any Decepticon—by surprise, he'd have immediately gone into a defensive mode, ready to do battle. His current situation, however, was far from normal.

He didn't *see* Starscream exactly. It was more like he felt him. Even bodiless, there was a certain arrogant feel to him.

Starscream? Is that you? Bluestreak thought-spoke.

So, Bluestreak, you're not dead, either, the Decepticon answered. *Just formless.*

That's me. As formless as a cloud.

And about as powerful, Starscream replied. *We both are.*

I don't know. Perhaps….

Perhaps what?

Perhaps if we work together, we can overpower this creature. Take him over, like he took us over.

Work together? Since when does a Decepticon need an Autobot's help.

Since one became bodiless, just like the other.

A fair point, Starscream admitted. *What do you suggest?*

A full-on mental assault. Everything we've got upstairs against everything he's got. And as busy as he is right now, maybe we'll have a chance.

Looking out through the newly formed visual receptors the alien had created, both of them chuckled. Optimus Prime, Megatron, Prowl, Skywarp and Soundwave were hammering at him with every weapon in their arsenal.

He is a bit busy, isn't he? Starscream said.

Just a bit.

In perfect accord, the two floated through the body of the Keeper, heading for what passed as its brain.

Bumblebee gathered up Spike, Paul and Franklin in his arms and ran for the far side of the platform. There were more explosives and weapons going off out there where Optimus and the others had engaged that bizarre meld of Starscream, Bluestreak and a Keeper than he'd ever seen at once. The Independence Day celebration in New York City had fewer explosions and lights.

Setting them down, he reached a decision. "Spike, if you're going to figure out how that thing works, now's the time. We can't leave and we can't stay. Maybe if you remove the threat of the Keepers, the military will detonate that weapon in the air instead of right here."

Spike clutched at the crystal, and nodded. "I'll...I'll try to remember."

"Good," Bumblebee said. "In the meantime, I'll try to keep you all alive." He scanned the area. "Which, for right now, looks like an easy task."

"Nothing's ever easy," Franklin said, pointing. "Take a look at that."

In the center of the lawn there was an extraordinarily deep crater. Likely, several bombs had exploded in the same location, each digging progressively deeper. Now, rising up out of the center of it were two things: Energon, the liquid silvery-yellow power source used by the Autobots and the Decepticons and...a tyrannosaurus rex, covered in Energon and looking *very* angry.

"Grimlock!" Bumblebee shouted. "You're alive!"

With a roar of triumph, the massive Dinobot climbed out of the ground.

"Oh, he's definitely alive," Franklin said, shoving Paul and Spike backward. "And he's *really* pissed off."

CHAPTER

TWENTY

The race that called themselves the Keepers had been floating through the universe for long eons. In their long history, their mental powers had been unmatched: they could read minds with ease, create weapons of destruction that would wipe out a planet, heal physical damage to themselves and others almost instantaneously, could create illusions so real that any who saw them believed what they saw *was* real. Driven by their nature to explore and learn, but constrained by their core programming that they *could not go* where they weren't invited, the Keepers had learned to be masters of trickery and false promises, using these as tools to gain access to new worlds and new races.

The Keepers did not know or had long ago forgotten who created them, techno-organic life-forms with the ability to adapt and dominate almost any obstacle they encountered. But they knew, and had once admitted to Optimus Prime, that deep in their core programming, they were limited, too, by a driving need to create *new* life, to evolve as the years passed...and they had been unable to do this.

Their fascination with the Transformers, who were

also living machines, stemmed from the fact that, to all appearances, they *did* in fact change. But change of self, or the rebuilding of a shell is not the same thing as creating life...new life. And, like the Keepers, the Transformers were unable to do this.

Never before, though, had the Keepers encountered anything like human beings. While many were like the hopeless sheep races that had fallen before, a few were extraordinarily strong-willed. Illusions shattered before them. Promises meant nothing. The human capacity for love and hate was unequaled anywhere that the Keepers had traveled. The passion of these special souls was almost limitless.

And that gave them power. The same power that resided in the Transformers, who were passionate defenders of all that might be termed good in the universe. While it was obvious to the Keepers that the humans and the Transformers regarded themselves very differently, in reality, they were not so different at all.

The reality of this world called Earth was that the forms adopted by the Keepers were subject to physical harm, and without form, they could wield no real power. And now, they had trapped themselves in a sphere within a sphere in a desperate effort to bring control back to the situation.

Even as they fought one of their own, who had somehow been mentally taken control of, their thoughts raced between them. The only conclusion they reached was that escape of some form must be accomplished...until the day they could return to this place and exact revenge on these passionate beings.

The Keepers had used trickery to gain access to this world, like so many others. From the depths of the

Earth, buried deep in the soil and rock, they called for a shard of crystal and with the power of their minds, they shaped it...and they called out to one who was susceptible to their will. One who had tasted a little power and wanted more. One who could be manipulated with technology or physiology. One who would do as he was told with the false promises whispered into his mind to keep him satisfied. One who could keep a secret, or a whole bevy of secrets.

The one who answered their call was already a little mentally unbalanced, which suited the Keepers purposes then...and now.

Dropping the shield from around the platform, the Keepers called out to their chosen disciple once more, their grasp on his mind hitting with the force of an iron spike.

And, as before, the illusory promises of power beyond his wildest imaginings proved too tempting to resist.

With barely a moment of hesitation, Franklin Townsend, NSA Agent, second-in-command of the organization known as the Followers, all-purpose opportunist and borderline psychotic, answered the Keepers' call.

Spike and Paul fell in a jumble of arms and legs when Franklin shoved them both out of the way of the path of the Dinobot Grimlock. The massive metal dinosaur, pulling itself out of a growing lake of pure Energon, called out a challenge to all those present. "Grimlock here! Grimlock destroy aliens! Grimlock destroy Decepticons!"

The sight and sound of the giant *T-rex* was enough to momentarily halt the battle between the bizarre

Keeper that had somehow melded the forms of Starscream and Bluestreak into one titanic alien built for killing and the aligned forces of Autobots and Decepticons swirling at its feet.

"Grimlock!" Optimus Prime yelled. Frantically gesturing at the others to move out of the way of the rampaging dinosaur, Prime jumped to one side.

Grimlock collided with the Keeper in a resounding crash. Roaring, his powerful jaws clamped down on one of its metal arms, tearing through cables and steel with ease. With a hard yank, he tore the arm—which bore a strong resemblance to one of Starscream's wing—free and tossed it aside.

The Keeper actually screamed, but as Spike watched, the missing limb began to regrow, welding itself together out of other pieces on the body frame of the alien.

"It *can* be hurt!" Prime yelled, then opened up with his own weapon. The others quickly followed suit, driving the Keeper backwards as it tried to fend off a virtual rain of deadly weapons in addition to a rampaging metal dinosaur.

After disentangling themselves, Spike and Paul struggled to their feet. "Jesus," Paul said, shaking his head. "That thing is...something."

Spike couldn't help himself. He started laughing. "That's one way to put it," he said. He bent down and picked up the crystal shard. "Hey," he said. "It's glowing."

The bluish-white crystal, which previously had held a faint inner light, was now glowing brightly. The strange markings on its side were now a reddish-orange color.

"Hey Franklin," Spike said, turning to the agent, "what do you make of this?"

Spike considered himself a fairly well-trained observer, but it would've taken a blind man not to notice that something was wrong with the NSA agent who was standing there, almost slack-jawed, his eyes far away. "Franklin?" Spike said, passing a hand in front of his face. "Are you all right?"

He turned to Paul, who was now staring at the platform on which the other Keepers were apparently battling amongst themselves. "Paul?" Spike said. "Something's wrong with—"

And that's when Franklin's head snapped up, and Spike, who was also fairly intuitive, realized that not only was something wrong, but that inside somewhere, Franklin had....snapped.

Spike just started to call out Bumblebee's name, when Franklin's arm reached out with incredible speed to make a snatch at the crystal. "Give it to me," he snarled.

Dancing backwards as fast as possible, Spike clutched the crystal tighter. He didn't know what was wrong with the man, but he did know one thing: there was no way in hell that he was giving him the crystal right now.

"I don't think that's a good idea," Spike said.

Franklin lunged forward, his augmented body moving with a grace that was nothing short of amazing. "Don't make me kill you, Spike," Franklin said. "I just want the crystal."

"What the hell's gotten into you?" Spike said, leaping out of the way just as Franklin jumped forward. Spike teetered on the edge of a crater in the lawn, caught his balance, and continued to back up.

"Give me the crystal!" Franklin yelled.

He's practically foaming at the mouth, Spike realized. *And where is Bumblebee?* He continued his backwards dance, now trying to circle to stay clear of the battle rampaging nearby and....on the platform, where that maniac Paul had somehow breached the barrier put up by the Keepers.

Franklin leaped forward again, his massive arms outstretched. "I'll have that crystal, Spike," he said. "*Now.*"

"Uh-uh," Spike said. Shooting for brevity, and desperately searching for Bumblebee, he added, "Not until you give me three references from qualified psychiatrists and promise you've taken your meds." *Optimus was right not to trust him*, Spike thought.

Suddenly, Franklin stopped pursuing him, an almost pensive grin on his face. "Spike," Franklin said. "Come on now, we've been through thick and thin. I don't want to hurt you, but I have to have the crystal."

Continuing to circle, Spike managed to put a fairly good-sized hole between them. "Okay, Franklin," Spike called. "I'll play along. Why do you have to have the crystal?"

"Because I know how to open the gate," he said. "I know how to send them back."

"Oh really," Spike said. "Because I sort of thought it was *me* that had to use the crystal."

Franklin shook his head. "I lied to you, Spike. I was the one using the crystal. It was me the whole time." He began making his way around the crater. "But I can't open the gate without touching the crystal first." He held out one meaty hand. "Give it to me and I'll send them back."

Spike shook his head. "Sorry buddy, but no can do. You don't seem like yourself right now." A beam of misdirected energy shot over their heads, and Spike ducked without thinking about it.

In that millisecond of inattention, Franklin was on him.

A solid right to the jaw spun Spike completely around. He stumbled, tried to correct himself, then fell into the bomb crater. Somehow, he managed to hold on to the crystal shard.

Franklin jumped in after him. He held out his hand again. "Give it to me, Spike," he said. "Don't make me hurt you."

Crab crawling backward, his jaw feeling like it had been battered with a hammer, Spike clutched the crystal even more tightly. His negative intention must have been obvious, because Franklin stepped forward and planted a snap kick to Spike's left shin.

Crack! Spike actually heard the bone snap before the pain hit him like a jolt of lightning. Then he screamed.

Using his one good leg, he somehow found the strength to continue pushing backward. His left leg was utter agony, and Spike could easily envision bone chips sawing back and forth like rusty teeth.

Franklin moved forward again. "Spike, I'll kill you if I must. Give me the crystal now."

Spike decided he hated this man. This man who had used him, had lied to him, had threatened to harm his family. Between gritted teeth, he hissed, "Over my dead body."

The agent smiled, and the psychotic gleam in his eye grew even brighter. "So be it," he said, and advanced once more.

Shoving himself backwards, trying to get up on his one good leg, didn't spare him more than a few seconds of pain. Franklin leaned down and grabbed Spike's broken shin. He could feel his bones grinding back and forth beneath the intensely strong grip of the augmented human. He tried not to scream again, but failed as the agent actually picked him up by the broken leg.

The pain was enormous, an icy pick of fire and teeth that shot through his leg and into his hip. Spike wanted to call out for Bumblebee, for Optimus, for *anybody*, but all that he could manage was a thin, whistling squeak.

Franklin lifted him up and tossed him down so hard, Spike felt the ground give way beneath him. What little breath was left in his body *wooshed* out of him. Another hard kick, this one to his right leg, about four inches above the knee.

Krr-Snap!

A wave of faintness passed over him, and Spike felt cold beads of sweat pop out on his brown in the brief second before this pain hit him. This was worse than his shin, a thousand times worse. This was the agony that poets in hell wrote about on their long journey across the barren wastelands of Satan's kingdom.

Hating himself, hating his weakness, Spike heard himself gibbering. "No more, no more, no more."

Franklin laughed. "It's too late for that, little man." He kicked Spike again, this time a playful tap that shot a fresh bolt of pain through him, but didn't break anything. "Now give me that goddamned crystal!"

Okay, you sonofabitch, Spike thought. He knew his lucid moments were fading rapidly, that he could pass out at almost any second. *Come and get it.* "Fine," Spike managed between gasps. "Fine. You win."

Spike held his arms out, the crystal clutched in his right hand like an offering. "Take the damn thing."

Franklin stepped forward, triumphant.

Bumblebee didn't want to leave Spike unprotected, but he did have the augmented human Franklin. Prime didn't trust him, but so far, he'd proven himself a reliable companion. The Energon continued to bubble up from beneath the ground.

Prime needs to know this, Bumblebee thought. Without a second's hesitation, he ran forward, ducking and weaving as bolts of energy, laser blasts, and close range mortars shattered the air and the ground. He followed in Grimlock's deeply imbedded footsteps, hoping to reach Optimus without getting himself killed.

The noise was horrendous, and as he neared where Optimus and Megatron were crouched side-by-side, hammering away at the Keeper, he had to yell to make himself heard. "Optimus!"

Turning away from the battle for a second, Prime looked deeply annoyed. "Why aren't you protecting Spike?"

Bumblebee waved the question away, though he hated disappointing his commander. "He's fine," Bumblebee shouted. "Look!" He pointed at the crater that Grimlock had risen out of. "It's pure Energon!"

Prime stared at the rising pool of their primary energy source, the energy that the Matrix used. "It...I haven't seen that much Energon in years," he said. "What's it doing here?"

"Who knows, who cares," Bumblebee yelled. "Does it help?"

Prime got to his feet. "More than you know," he said. "Good work, Bumblebee. Now get back to Spike." Without another word, Prime headed for the pool at top speed.

Bumblebee smiled, happy to have been able to help in some small way. He turned to head back to where Spike, Franklin and Paul had been crouched when he noticed that all three were gone. A quick scan put Paul....in the middle of the Keepers, blasting away at them for all he was worth.

But where were Spike and Franklin?

And that's when he heard Spike scream in such agony that the noise of it carried over the sounds of the battle.

What have I done? Bumblebee thought. Then he bolted as fast as he'd ever run before in his life to find and help his friend Spike.

TWENTY-ONE

*T*he buildings were literally exploding around them. Chunks of concrete the size of cars fell from the sky to slam into the ground. Fires burned as gas mains ruptured and exploded. A good portion of the city was burning.

Overhead, Transformers fought in the sky. Wire-guided missiles whistling between them, and shattering the air with deafening booms.

Melony ran, dragging her sister Jenny along behind her. "Come on!" she screamed. "We've got to move!"

Suddenly, Jenny stumbled, almost fell and dragged Melony down with her. "Damn it!" Melony yelled when she lost her grip. "Jenny, get your—"

The building across the street from them burst. The shock wave from the blast throwing Melony backwards as she hauled Jenny back to her feet. A twisted chunk of steel, mortar, bone and other elements the size of her daddy's old Buick smashed into the ground next to her, chewed through the asphalt sidewalk and exploded the window behind her. Shards of glass flew in all directions, but none touched her.

Shaking her ringing head, Melony got back to her

feet and saw Jenny. She screamed her sister's name and ran to her. She knelt, staring down at the ruin of her sister's body. Glass shards the size of swords jutted from her chest, her stomach, her throat.

Melony felt the emotion drain out of her, the physician in her assessing the damage as she'd been trained to do. Her sister was dead—that was a certainty. Overhead, the battle raged on and she felt a cold rage wash over her. A dark hatred that consumed her in an instant, an emotional tidal wave that engulfed her whole being....but never passed on.

The Keeper, Melony realized. He's trying to use my memories to imprison me.

She screamed again, knowing it was useless, knowing that the Transformers cared nothing for her loss. They were as indifferent as the stars, as untouchable as gods.

Melony forced herself to pull away from the memory. It didn't matter, she assured herself. All that mattered now was the Keepers who were worse than the Transformers. Who had taken her body when that's all she really had left.

As she mentally drifted away from the scene, she saw something that was new. The Keeper had exposed her memories completely, not as she saw them through her own eyes, but as her *mind* had seen....and refused to see.

Kneeling on the street, cradling her sister's body, hating....hating them for being so much bigger and stronger than the frail human life that lay wasted at her feet. It should have been her. She's the one who'd been selfish. Why hadn't the flying glass taken her?

On the street behind her, unseen in her emotional

turmoil, stands a small, yellow Autobot. His face is sad, his compassion evident. He brushes hunks of glass out of his armor, then, shaking his head ruefully, he turns to leave her to her own grief, not wanting to interrupt. He transforms into a yellow Volkswagon Bug, and races down the street.

He was *behind* me, Melony realizes. He….he *saved* me. And I hated them all for it.

The Keeper, suddenly aware that the memory would only empower her to fight harder, tried to shut it off. Melony mentally slapped him back down.

This is my body now! You owe me that!

They will destroy us both! the Keeper cried out.

Good, Melony thought. *It's the least I can do.*

She returned her thoughts to the battle at hand. The Keepers were awkward and clumsy at hand-to-hand combat, the new forms they'd chosen for this life unfamiliar to them. She slashed at them with the blades of her arms, slicing at cables and gears and metal plating.

Forcing herself forward, Melony screamed a mental war cry. *This is for Jenny! This is for Paul!* Lunge-slash-parry-slash. *This is for the Transformers!*

Though obviously not well-suited to this kind of fighting, the Keepers gave back in force, damaging the body of the one who had been called The Voice, while healing their own as fast as she could harm them.

I cannot live to hate anymore, Melony realized. *I have done wrong by myself and by them. Would that I could tell Paul about this…perhaps he'd find it in his heart to forgive me for wronging him. Perhaps he'd even find a way to forgive himself.*

And then...he was there.

Paul got to his feet after Franklin shoved him and Spike to the ground. He hadn't a clue how Grimlock had gotten down there, but it seemed like any help they could get on *this* side of the barrier would be a good thing...and Grimlock was a *big*-sized help. He glanced back at the platform where the Keepers were still fighting amongst themselves.

The barrier of energy they'd erected around themselves seemed almost impervious to force, and Paul gritted his teeth in frustration. He had to get past it, he had to if he wanted to do the one thing he'd come here to accomplish.

And then, as though some strange god had heard and capriciously decided to grant his request, the barrier flickered once and vanished. *Now!* Paul thought, leaping onto the platform and drawing his weapon. He ran across the wooden slats, ignoring the battle on the lawn below, his mind intent on one thing: killing the one that had once been a woman called Melony.

Sliding to a stop beyond their huddled forms, Paul was reminded at first of a snake pit. Cables and wires writhed about, lashing through the air with a *hissing-snap* sound that was eerily reminiscent of a striking rattler. But there was far more danger here than in any reptile of the earth. Metal blades whirred to and fro as the Keepers fought each other. Sharpened spikes the size of baseball bats gouged the air and anything within reach.

And near the center of it all, Paul could make out the horribly altered form of Melony. Her face was bloodied, her new form scorched and damaged, but repairs were seemingly underway. No emotion crossed her features, the only sounds on the platform the *ping* of metal against metal, the crunch and grind of gears.

All of the Keepers seemed intent on destroying a single one of them, which was fighting for all it was worth. They completely ignored his presence.

Paul drew his 9mm Glock from its holster, tapped the laser sight, and took careful aim. A small red dot, the size of a quarter at this distance, appeared on Melony's forehead. He didn't want to do it, didn't want to destroy all that remained of her. The dot wavered slightly.

But she was dead, Paul reminded himself. She was *dead*—and he'd promised himself that he'd save her.

This was about the best he could do. The dot steadied, and Paul gently squeezed the trigger.

The gun was loaded with hollow-point bullets, and this one entered the Keeper's head with enough velocity to rock the entire skull structure backwards. It exited, leaving a hole about the size of a coffee saucer. A bizarre mix of blood and wires and bone hitting the Keeper behind it with a wet splat.

Melony's eyes—*the Keeper's eyes*, Paul reminded himself—rolled back in its head. He fired again, catching it almost directly between her—*its!*—eyes.

The Keeper—Melony—fell over backward and hit the platform with a heavy thud.

For a second, silence shrouded the platform. *Wow*, thought Paul. *All those weapons we brought here. Who would've thought a trusty 9mm to the head would do the job?*

Then the dead Keeper on the platform began to stir.

Or not, thought Paul.

With a clanking of metal, several of the Keepers turned to face him.

Well, at least they know I'm here now. Paul targeted the closest one and opened fire. His aim was precise, and for most creatures, would have been deadly.

Every shot was placed in a critical area—heads, if he could tell where the head was. Otherwise, he aimed for joints, guessing that the heavy metal plating they'd scavenged for armor was most susceptible there. He was not wrong, as several times they had to stop and heal themselves.

He went through two clips before he was in the midst of them. And even as the first blade struck home, Paul dropped the now useless gun and continued to lash out, yanking on cables with all his strength, jerking wires and pulling on appendages.

He felt the blade sink into his lower back, and cried out in pain. It missed his spine, though, and Paul gritted his teeth and snared another cable with his strong hands, pulling it free in a shower of sparks.

Despite the pain, despite his failure, Paul suddenly realized that he was....happy. *At least I'm doing something*, he thought. *I'm doing something that matters. Not just to me, not just to my silly quest to understand God, to have faith....but something that matters to the whole world. I'm fighting for everyone.*

It was an exhilarating sensation, and a momentary, renewed strength flowed through his limbs even as another blade buried itself in his abdomen. A burning pain lashed at him, but he kept on. Slower now, then he had been, but still fighting.

It's okay, he told himself. *It's okay because I finally get it. I'm through running. The Father was wrong. I don't have to understand God to believe in Him. Every*

*conscious living being, even the Transformers, must
have a god, I bet. Maybe even more than one. Though
I don't suppose I'll ever get the chance to ask them.*

It's okay to fail, Paul realized with a jolt. *As long
as you try to do what's right, what is best.* And he'd
always done that.

Another bunch of wires tore loose in his scrabbling
fists as a third blade cut across the back of his legs,
cutting through both his hamstrings. Unable to stand,
Paul fell forward into the arms of the Keeper that the
others had been trying to kill.

And then the strangest thing happened. He
could....*feel* Melony, could hear her voice in his mind
as clearly as if she were standing beside him.

Paul, she said. *I'm safe. You kept your promise. You
saved me.*

An image of the humans that had been trapped on
the Keepers' world flashed through his mind.

You saved us all.

I did?

Yes, she said. Her voice was so soft, so gentle, so
soothing that he barely noticed the pain of the blades
now cutting into him from all directions.

You can rest now, Paul, she said. *All your failures,
like mine, were all too human. And God forgives those.
Just like you've forgiven me...and I've forgiven the
Transformers.*

*That's so good to hear, Melony. You're a much more
special person than you give yourself credit for.*

Paul could feel her smile, but he couldn't see it. He
didn't have to. It was the first real smile she'd ever
offered him, but he knew it would light up a room
like a Christmas tree.

Thank you, Paul, Melony said. *Thank you for everything.*

You...you're welcome, Melony, Paul said.

Paul's vision flared—a bright, blinding white light that filled his senses. And he plunged into it and never looked back.

CHAPTER

TWENTY-TWO

Engaged as he was in trying to kill the Keeper who had become a horrific combination of Starscream and Bluestreak, Megatron paid little attention when Bumblebee came up and began frantically talking to Optimus Prime. The mighty Grimlock, a prehistoric killing machine built with advanced technology was currently doing his best to disassemble the Keeper, while Megatron and the others continued to throw a barrage of weaponry at it.

Then Optimus stood up and began to run *away* from the battle. And this didn't suit Megatron's plans at all. He jumped to his feet and ran after Optimus, his eyes immediately seeing the rising pool of Energon.

He reached the edge of the Energon-filled crater just seconds behind Optimus Prime, who was staring down into the pool with a look of deep thought on his face.

"Do you have any ideas for that?" Megatron asked.

Prime nodded. "One, but I don't know if it will work."

"Sometimes being a leader is all about guessing,"

Megatron said. "And we're at the point where guesses is all we've really got."

"I know," Optimus said. "But if I'm wrong…"

"Then you'll be wrong," Megatron snarled. "It certainly won't be the *first* time, will it?"

"No," Optimus said. "It wouldn't." He opened his chest plate and removed the Matrix. "My thought is that the Matrix is an artifact of immense power. Even after having held it for so long, I do not know all its abilities or functions. I do know that it holds the wisdom and knowledge of all those who were Prime before me, and will hold mine when I am gone." He gestured at the Keeper fighting behind them. "On their world, the power of the Matrix hurt them. And there they had an advantage, even though its power surprised them. Here, I think a different solution is called for…. I just don't know what, exactly, it will do."

Megatron, who'd just noticed a human doing battle on the platform with the Keepers, and was about to bring this to Optimus' attention, opened his mouth to say that at least one of the barriers was down for some reason, when Optimus leaped *into* the pool of Energon.

"What the…" Megatron said, his voice trailing off in surprise.

In the pool, Optimus immediately began to sink, the Matrix held out before him like an offering to some Cybertronian god. Already, his stalwart form was encased in a silvery-yellow light as the Energon contained in the Matrix flowed over him and began to interact with the Energon in the pool. A wave of pure-radiance erupted out of the crater, almost blinding Megatron, who shielded his eyes.

"I *hate* it when he does that," Megatron snarled under his breath.

The wave of light passed over him, and suddenly the dome of energy surrounding them was an opaque ocean of silver and white, brighter than full afternoon sunlight. The Decepticons and Autobots engaged in fighting the Keeper paused momentarily to glance at this new phenomenon—wondering, no doubt, if it was some new power of the Keepers about to descend on them.

Though he knew that the Matrix could only be contained by one named Prime, Megatron also knew something else: if the Autobot's didn't have it, their power would be greatly diminished.

When Optimus landed in the Energon pool, his biggest fear was that somehow the Matrix could be overloaded. Like a backfiring weapon or an engine pushed to fear, Optimus wondered if the Matrix wouldn't try to absorb *all* the Energon present and simply…self-destruct. And likely take all of them with it.

Instead, however, the Matrix pulsed in his hands, and Optimus felt his armor and his systems…changing. The glowing liquid quickly covered his legs, his torso, his arms, and as he sank beneath the surface, strangely unafraid, he knew that something else was happening. Something he'd never before imagined or experienced, let alone could it have been predicted.

He could feel the Energon seeping into his circuits and processors, coating them in its power. *How am I changing?* Optimus thought.

You are becoming something more than you were, a stern, but not unkind voice answered.

Suddenly, Optimus saw him. Sentinel Prime. A regal form of blue, gold and silver armor, with eyes of white. His forerunner as Prime and the one who had so recently battled him on the Keepers' world.

Have you come to mock me yet again? Optimus asked him. *Why do you haunt me so?*

I have not come to mock you, Optimus. I appeared to you in Tokyo when you needed to call forth the strength of deep, personal anger to defend yourself against Megatron. The Keepers generated me from your own memories on their world, to see how you would fare against one who came before you. You are Prime, Optimus. I come to you because when you are in danger, the Matrix senses your need and calls me, and sometimes others, forth to offer guidance.

Other than the obvious, what danger am I in now? Optimus wondered.

Engulfing yourself and the Matrix in pure Energon is danger enough, Sentinel said. *The Keepers call Energon the Source. They fear it, as they do no other substance in the universe. For their powers cannot affect it. It is one of the reasons they chose this place to come to—for in studying Energon, they had hoped to harness its power.*

Like they need more, Optimus thought sourly.

Now comes the most difficult time for you, Optimus, Sentinel said. *When you leave the pool, it will feel as though you have been reborn. For a time, you will have powers unlike any you have ever held before. This event will surely mark you, change you—a new Prime for a new age. But what kind of Prime you will be is up to you. I beseech you—follow the path of honor and right. Do not be led down the path of battle for the sake*

*of the battle itself, though we were built for such uses.
We are the defenders of all that is right in the universe,
Optimus. Even when defending what is right, or doing
what honor demands, costs us or our loved ones, all
we hold dear. To do less than follow the path of honor
is to spit in the eye of our proud history.*

As quickly as he'd appeared, Sentinel was gone.
Encased in Energon, Optimus spared one more
moment to reflect on what Sentinel had said, and to
review his Energon-enhanced systems. He had never
felt so powerful, so strong. So certain of the path he
must take, what he must do.

Optimus smiled to himself. He was Prime, and it
was time to end this.

He kicked for the surface.

Staring into the pool, wondering what exactly was
about to happen, Megatron jumped backwards in
surprise as what appeared Optimus Prime shot out
of the liquid with the speed of a laser. The form was
essentially the same, but in an instant, Megatron could
tell that he'd somehow changed. The Energon had
reacted with Prime's armor and the Matrix in a completely unexpected way.

His armor plating, once red, blue and white, was
now a shining blanket of silver and yellow. In the
glowing light, the crevices appeared a deep, velvety
blue, though it may have been a trick of the shadows.
Vaguely seen Cybertronian symbols, much like those
on the Matrix which was still clutched in Optimus'
mighty fists, shimmered in the air around him. All
the damage that had been done in the battles on the
Keepers' world, and in this battle, was gone.

This was an Optimus restored and then some. His

demeanor was that of a determined general, prepared to die for his cause. He landed next to Megatron, his eyes glowing with the clear light of knowledge.

"What happened in there?" Megatron demanded. "What happened to you?"

For a moment, Optimus looked at him, almost into him it seemed, and then he said, "I know what must be done, Megatron. I will honor our agreement, but for now you must stand aside."

The voice and presence were so commanding that Megatron stepped out of the way without conscious thought, and by the time he realized what he was doing, it was too late to stop himself.

His shining armor gleaming, Optimus strode without pause or fear across the battlefield. "Autobots!" he called out, his voice so loud that it carried over the noise of the weapons and clanking bodies of the Keepers. "Autobots, cease fire!"

Prowl, Jazz, Iron Hide, and Sunstreaker all looked up from their weapons at this new Optimus Prime.

"To me," Optimus said. "Form a circle."

They ran across the lawn to do as he'd commanded, and Megatron immediately ordered the Decepticons to withdraw as well. As they gathered around, asking questions, he snarled, "I don't *know* what he's doing."

The Keeper who had altered Starscream and Bluestreak did not advance, obviously taking advantage of the lull to repair itself once again, shaping and reforming metal parts and pieces to create stronger joints and better armor plating.

Optimus was quite an astonishing sight, his armor glowing and newly formed. "Where's Bumblebee?" he asked Prowl.

"He took off over there," Prowl said, gesturing towards the platform. "But I don't see him now."

Optimus frowned. "I don't have time to deal with that right now. The warhead will be here in minutes."

He held out his arms, and the Autobots drew close. A stirring of jealousy rumbled through Megatron's circuits. His own Decepticons did not follow him this loyally, would never exhibit this kind of trust. The price, he supposed, for leading the lives they did.

"I do not have time to explain it all to you now," Optimus told them. "But I have been given a gift from the Matrix. For a brief time, I will be…more than I was before." He motioned towards his altered armor. "Perhaps when all this is over, if I am successful, I will be able to explain it to you."

A chorus of protests followed this statement, and Optimus shook his head. "No, my friends. Not now. I must ask you to put your faith in me, in the Matrix, in the wisdom of those who came before us and taught us to do what is right and honorable. With that faith, and your help, we will defeat the Keepers."

"How?" Prowl said. "So far, nothing's done more than temporarily annoy them."

"I know," Optimus said. "But that will change." He raised the Matrix up overhead, and turned to Megatron. "When the barrier comes down, call for Devastator and Omega Sentinel. Call on Laserbeak and Buzzsaw. Prowl, you will call for Ratchet and Wheeljack. They will only have a few moments to get here. Do you understand?"

"We have few choices," Megatron said. "Yes, I understand."

"As you command," Prowl said.

"Autobots, you must join hands, each holding onto

the next. Two of you must be on either side of me, holding onto my waist."

Jazz and Sunstreaker stepped forward. "What about Grimlock?" Jazz asked.

The Dinobot had not come forward to join with the others, though he had retreated from the Keeper and was watching the proceedings with interest. "That is up to him," Optimus said. "He has always been a part of us, if he so chooses."

"I choose," Grimlock said, transforming into his robot form. "I choose new Optimus." He walked forward and joined hands with the others.

"Now," Optimus said. "We will do what must be done." He closed his eyes, and the Matrix began to pulsate and flare.

He's more powerful than ever before, Megatron thought. *But will it be enough?*

Optimus Prime silently called on his ancestors for strength, and queried the Matrix held high over his head. *What is this power? What are its limits?*

A tool, a wish. It is what you make of it.

Optimus immediately recognized the voice the Matrix had chosen. Alpha Trion. Would he ever be as wise? *What may I make of it?*

There are few incidents in our long history of a Prime in possession of the Matrix being engulfed in Energon. It has healed you, even changed you for a time, but be warned: this power, this...gift may only be used once, Alpha Trion warned him. *Going down this path again would likely lead to your destruction. It is the power of Energon multiplied in strength and possibility. It can kill, it can grant life. It can be wis-*

*dom or folly, kindness or cruelty. It can harness energy
and release it as a weapon, it can create shelter from
the storm. It is the penultimate power of being Prime.*

Optimus consider the situation they were in. The
Keepers would win should he not defeat them.
Thousands, perhaps millions would die, should the
nuclear weapon strike. It was possible that Spike had
already failed or been betrayed by Franklin and the
gate would not be opened. One thing was certain…he
must act.

How long will the power last? Prime asked.

As long as you do, Alpha Trion said. *Its strength
and purpose are linked to yours.*

Prime felt the burden of leadership upon him, but
he could also feel the faith the Autobots had in his
strength. Even the Decepticons were trusting him to
save them. One of the chief ironies of his life was that
killing still abhorred him.

What will you do with the power? Alpha Trion
asked.

I will do what I must, answered Prime. *What honor
demands.*

And then he decided.

The Keeper who had so horribly altered Starscream
and Bluestreak saw the Autobot known as Optimus
Prime, the one who had hurt them so terribly, come
out of the pool covered in the silver radiance of the
source.

His brethren were still entangled in a battle of will
and flesh on the platform, so no help was forthcoming
from them. Suddenly, those who had been attacking
him retreated and gathered near Optimus Prime.

The Keeper knew this would be his one chance to

destroy them all. A moment given to repairs, and then he would encase them with his powers all at once. He began directing the repairs when he felt the first jolt that something was wrong. Something, someone was....in his mind. Like the others would be only....there was no sense of sharing. Only a sense of anger.

Hello, you disgusting piece of slag, a voice called into his mind. *I think you've about run out of escape routes.*

Who are you? the Keeper said, frantically trying to locate the being.

We are Bluestreak, we are Starscream, the voice said. *And you...are...finished!*

The pain was so intense that the Keeper screamed aloud. It felt as though this BlueStar being was driving a metal pick into his mind over and over again.

Get out! Get out! Get out of my mind! he screamed. Across the field, the Decepticons watched with interest as the Keeper gibbered and danced, flailing wildly about.

Sorry, but thanks to you we've just got nowhere else to go!

The mental ice pick rammed home again, and the Keeper clutched at what passed for his skull. *It's them*, he realized. *The one's I combined. The transformation must have released them from their prisons.*

No, Bluestreak and Starscream corrected. *We released ourselves.*

The Keeper felt his logic circuits and servomotors freezing up. He tried to get his body to respond to his mental commands, but the joints were as frozen as blocks of ice. *I'll release you*, he promised them.

I'll reform you, rebuild you better than before. Just...let...me...go! This last was a rising note of hysteria, a scream of pure anguish.

Not in a thousand, million years, they said.

And the ice pick became a dagger, then a sword, then a massive blade of pain and light driving the Keeper into a mental retreat he had never before experienced. Once, briefly, he called out for his brethren....but they had problems of their own.

CHAPTER

TWENTY-THREE

Blasts of pure Energon, white and silver, leapt from the encircled Autobots, into Optimus Prime, and from there into the pulsing cube of the Matrix. The artifact began to hum, a low sound that was somehow pleasing to the ear. More energy poured forth from them, as they fed their strength and energy to their cause. They retained enough for themselves to keep functioning at a bare minimum level, but little more. All of them but Optimus fell to the ground, unable to continue to stand.

Their energy, their faith poured into him and he held it, stoked it as a blacksmith stokes a fire, and in turn gave it to the Matrix. The glow about the device was so bright now it looked like he was holding onto a star. The energy contained within it so powerful that had his will been weaker, Optimus would have dropped it.

With a sudden flash, the Matrix sent a burst of energy at the barrier erected by the Keepers. It slammed into it and shattered through it in a millisecond to charge on into the night sky like a searchlight.

On the other side of the barrier, Devastator and

Omega Sentinel didn't need to be called…. They saw the barrier disappear and rushed across the lawn, each intent on the destruction of what he saw: Bluestreak and Starscream. They slammed into the Keeper with a horrendous crash, prepared to dismantle it piece by piece if that's what it took.

Down the Strip, Ratchet saw the radiance and knew it for a signal to return to Optimus. That he was needed there even more than he was needed here. He moved down the street at considerable speed to join the others.

In the night sky, Wheeljack, Laserbeak and Buzzsaw saw the beam of Energon blast through the clouds at almost the same moment they detected the incoming nuclear warhead. Each in his own turn considered running, but opted instead for the warm light of the Energon blazing out of Las Vegas. Better to die among friends and even foes one recognizes than to be alone and without either.

Optimus saw the barrier shatter and could actually feel the other Autobots and Decepticons approaching the area. They had only seconds before the warhead was going to hit, and Optimus knew that they were all going to die. Not even the Keepers could survive a nuclear blast at ground zero.

And that was why he had chosen to destroy the barrier. With the power of the Matrix and the Silver Coat, he might have been able to kill the Keepers or he might not. Perhaps he would not have been able to move quickly enough to destroy them before their turned their combined might on him.

Better to die, to let the Autobots die, to let so many humans die….if it virtually guaranteed the death of the Keepers as well. The path of honor and right was strewn with bodies. Wayside casualties who had died when those who would lead had been forced to make difficult choices. I am content, Optimus thought.

Ratchet ran up, ignoring the two gigantic Decepticons destroying what appeared to be an immobile Keeper. "Optimus, what's going on?" he asked.

"The end," Optimus said.

Across the lawn, Wheeljack and the two Decepticons landed and moved to join them.

Optimus' sensors picked up the incoming missile. It would be here in approximately ninety seconds.

Bumblebee peered over the edge of the crater where Spike's scream had come from. Below, his worst fears were realized. *Optimus was right not to trust him!* The human called Franklin had assaulted Spike—even from here, Bumblebee could see that Spike's legs were broken.

And he was holding out the crystal like an offering.

With a snarl of outrage, Bumblebee jumped into the crater, smashing his fists into Franklin's back with enough force to shatter a normal human's spine. Franklin collapsed on top of Spike, who cried out once in utter agony, then rolled away. He got to his feet about three or four yards away.

Embedded in his chest was the crystal.

"You're not human," Bumblebee said, standing over the now unconscious Spike.

"I prefer to think of it as *extra*-human," Franklin said. He reached out and plucked the shard from his chest. A gush of blood streamed from the wound, sputtered and then stopped. "I'm an augment," he said. "Not as tough as you Autobots, but I can hold my own."

Bumblebee refused to move away from Spike, though every circuit he had strained to pummel Franklin into the dirt.

"Why are you trying to hurt Spike?" Bumblebee said. "He's....he's a good person."

Franklin shrugged. "I have no interest in hurting Spike," he said. "I only wanted this." He held the crystal aloft. He turned his head slightly, as though listening to a voice in his ear. "And now that I have it, I'll be on my way."

There was no good that could come of this...thing having the crystal, Bumblebee knew, but he steeled himself. On the ground at his feet, blood trickled from the corner of Spike's mouth. "I won't try to stop you," Bumblebee said. "I can't leave Spike."

"Works for me," Franklin said. He leapt up and out of the pit with an agility far greater than any normal human possessed.

Bumblebee knelt on the ground next to his friend. "I'm so sorry, Spike," he said. "I shouldn't have left you." Afraid to move him, and afraid not to, Bumblebee jumped back up to the rim of the pit.

In the lawn, an Optimus he had never seen before had gathered the others near him. Over his head, he held the Matrix. It pulsed with its own light, and for a second, Bumblebee forgot all about Spike. The scene was....beautiful. Energy poured from the other Autobots into this new Prime, and from him into the Matrix. A low hum sounded and then suddenly a burst of energy from the Matrix shot into the sky and shattered the energy barrier erected by the Keepers.

There's no time left, Bumblebee realized. *That warhead will be here any second*. He jumped back down into the crater and returned to Spike's side. "I don't know what's going to happen, Spike," Bumblebee whispered. "But I do know one thing. I won't let *anything* else hurt you."

Feeling sorry that he'd let his friend and his commander down, Bumblebee did the only thing he could for now. He transformed into car mode and ever so slowly and carefully pulled over the top of Spike's unconscious form. Making an adjustment, he *encased* Spike inside his own protective armor.

"There," he said. "Let's hope my armor is shield enough for whatever happens next."

Clearing the top of the crater, Franklin made a beeline for the platform. The Keepers voices in his mind were almost screaming. *Hurry! Hurry! You must open the gate to get your reward!*

Bruised by the violent force of Bumblebee's fists and gouged from the crystal, Franklin still made good time across the battlefield. Behind him, a flare of white light shot into the sky, but he ignored it. *Keep moving,* he told himself. *There's no time for fooling around. It will be here any minute.*

Am I thinking that, Franklin wondered. Or the Keepers? It didn't matter, he supposed.

He reached the platform and climbed up the side, the crystal clenched in his fist. On top, the Keepers milled about, thrashing and fighting the one that had been called The Voice. It was horribly damaged now and didn't appear to be healing itself as the others would have done. Nearby, Franklin saw Paul's body. It had been thoroughly shredded by various sharp objects.

So much for the hero, Franklin thought.

Hurry! The Keepers ordered in voices so loud

Franklin wondered if he'd go deaf. *There's only seconds left.*

Franklin clutched the crystal in his fist, concentrating on the instructions he'd received. It was all a matter of will, he knew. All the Keepers powers were based on what others *believed* they could do, what they *believed* they saw. The Keepers were *very* strong-willed. I am very strong willed, Franklin thought. I have played the game well. I deserve to be rewarded

Yes! the Keepers hissed. *You will be rewarded if you open the gate.*

The shard began to glow with an internal light of its own. On its side, the strange markings pulsed and throbbed to the same rhythm as Franklin's heartbeat.

"I am strong," Franklin said aloud. "I can do conquer the universe!"

Without warning, the Keeper who had been The Voice slammed into him. Somehow, he managed to retain his hold on the crystal. Focus was everything he knew at this moment, and he would not allow his effort to fail.

The voices of the Keepers shrieked in outrage and converged on the traitor, and Franklin could hear them in his mind:

Kill it! Kill it before it destroys us all!

Hurry!

He knows about the source, hurry!

The bomb is coming, you must go faster!

And then a new voice, soft and feminine, and so very tired and so very hurt. *You've already lost*, she said. *And you don't even know it. Go ahead, Franklin. Open the gate. You deserve your reward....as do I.*

Yes I do, he thought. And so he did.

Optimus tracked the incoming missile with his sensors. No doubt the others were, too. *I am content*, he thought. *I have done what is right, though it costs so very much.*

On the platform, the human Franklin was surrounded by the Keepers who had, until moments ago, been fighting among themselves.

In the sky, Optimus could see the warhead coming into their position. A shrill, whistling sound preceded it, and Optimus wondered what it would feel like, if he would feel anything at all. *I have been a good Prime. I have done well by them.*

Yes, you have, he heard Sentinel say. *You have done very well indeed.*

On the platform an odd light appeared, flashed, and then a gate opened.

The warhead impacted the earth with a horrendous echoing boom, its energies released in nanoseconds.

The Matrix flared once more, as though sensing its demise.

A solid wave of energy washed over Prime, bringing him to his knees. For reasons unknown to him, he continued to hold the Matrix above his head. It flared again, and almost every last erg of energy shot out of Prime and into the artifact.

A silver net whipped into being, encircled the energy from the nuclear warhead, and spun into the platform.

The Keepers screeched in dismay and for one split-second, Prime saw a look of dismay on Franklin's face. Then he and the Keepers were sucked through the gate. Directly behind them, the energy of the Matrix net and the nuclear warhead followed them in.

A gigantic vortex of purple and green and crimson fire burst from the gate, spiraling outwards and burning the platform to cinders. Some kind of backlash, Prime thought. The Matrix flared once more and a silver glow encircled him and the Autobots around him, and all of the Decepticons but Omega Sentinel and Devastator. When the fire raced across Prime and the others, it passed harmlessly, repelled by the amazing energy of the Matrix.

Omega Sentinel and Devastator were not so lucky. But neither was the Keeper they had been tearing to pieces. *The price*, Optimus realized, *for the Matrix saving Decepticons in addition to Autobots.*

The wave of nuclear fire spread outwards, catching several buildings, and eventually dissipating. Perhaps contact with the Matrix's energy had weakened it somehow. On the platform, the gate flickered once and closed.

Optimus rose to his feet, exhausted, and replaced the Matrix in his chest cavity. Already, the effects on his armor were fading, his normal colors of red, blue and white slowly returning. Around him, Megatron and the others were also getting to their feet. His own Autobots lay quiet. They would need Energon to regain their strength.

He staggered in the direction of where he had last seen Bumblebee going. In a deep crater, he found him. Bumblebee, like Omega Sentinel and Devastator, had not been protected by the Matrix. A profound sorrow filled his heart.

This, too, is the price, he thought. *Sometimes those we care about most are lost....*

He made his way into the pit. "Bumblebee?" he said softly.

The little yellow car was scorched and blackened. Prime could see where the metal had literally been melted away to fry the circuits and servomotors below. "Bumblebee?" he said again.

"Ppp…ppprime," Bumblebee said.

Optimus dropped to one knee. "Easy now," he said. "We'll get you fixed up in no time."

"Hah…hhah," the always cheerful robot said. "Nnnot…this…tttime."

"Shhh," Optimus said.

"Sp…sppike," Bumblebee said. "Unn…unnder…neath me."

As gently as he would touch a butterfly, Prime lifted the little yellow car. Underneath lay Spike—broken and battered, but still very much alive.

"You saved him, Bumblebee," Optimus said. "You saved him."

"Gah…good enough," Bumblebee stuttered. "Al…always wanted to be a…hero."

"You are, Bumblebee," Optimus said. "You always have been."

He sat with Bumblebee then, one hand on the little car, the other cradling the injured Spike. They said nothing. There was nothing they needed to say.

When the sun crested the horizon, Bumblebee's last circuits shorted out, and the lights faded from his eyes.

Would that all of us could be so brave, Optimus thought. *What a world that would be.*

CHAPTER

TWENTY-FOUR

Allister watched the sun rise over the cornfields. It was a sight to behold as each leaf and stalk was outlined in gold and red, with dark silhouettes of green. He'd cracked a window earlier, and as the dew began to evaporate, a rich, lush smell filled the air. That's why he'd chosen to live here. The soil was good. It was a place for growing things.

On the other side of the limo, the vice president and his two Secret Service agents sat in silence. They didn't appear to appreciate the sunrise or the wonderful smell of growing things any more than one of those Keepers would. The Autobots, he was certain, would've appreciated it.

"I think we've waited long enough," the Vice President said. "Let's reestablish a channel."

One of the agents fiddled with the small television, turning it back on and adjusting the picture quality. On the screen, Allister could see that the room was in chaos.

"Mr. President," the vice president said. "What's going on?"

Waving his arms, he snarled, "Ask them! The military geniuses!"

"Sir?"

"Nothing happened as far as we can tell," the President said, slamming his fist onto the table. "It went off, we know that, but nothing *happened*." On the screen, live satellite images of the city of Las Vegas showed it burning in a few places, the buildings of the Strip utterly annihilated, but for the most part standing.

"I don't understand," the vice president said.

"Well, you're sure as hell not the only one in that particular crowd," the President said. Behind him, several of the generals were shouting at each other and pointing to another monitor. "Now what?" the President said.

"Mr. President, sir," one of the generals said. "It's Los Angeles. It's back."

"Back? Back from where?"

"We don't know sir, but an overflight of F-14s just reported that the black cloud that had covered it has...vanished." He pointed at the monitor. "There's some devastation from what looks like populace panic, but it's still there."

"Has *anything* gone right about this?" the president demanded. "I want an explanation, and I want it right God damn now!"

The chairman of the joint chiefs cleared his throat. "I can guess, if you'd like, sir."

"Then by all means guess," the President said.

"We've got satellite footage of some sort of....energy beam coming out of Las Vegas in the seconds before the nuke hit. At a guess, I'd say the Transformers found a way to defeat the Keepers and stop the nuke." He was doing his level best to not smile, but it was obvious that this pleased him.

"You're saying you think the Transformers stopped this?"

"Most likely the Autobots, sir," he said. "They're the good guys."

"Oh, for Christ's sake," the president said. He turned to the monitor. "I'm not done with you yet, Mr. Greaves. When I get this unraveled, you and I are going to have a meeting of the minds."

Allister smiled. The president, too, had some skeletons in his closet. Some Dinobot-sized ones. "Of course, Mr. President," he said smoothly. "But for now, I've got an organization to run."

"Take him home," the president said shortly, then cut the connection.

The vice president never said another word on the drive back to Allister's house. The car stopped in the drive, and Allister stepped out. Before walking away, he leaned back into the car and said, "I hope you don't mind, Mr. Vice President, but I wanted to let you know something."

"What's that?" he asked sullenly.

"You remember that girl in Topeka, the one who was "almost eighteen" but not quite?" Allister asked.

The vice president's face went ashen, but he didn't speak or even nod.

"If you *ever* harm one of my people again, I'll make sure the media gets full documentation, which I happen to have several copies of."

"You sonofabitch," the vice president said.

"Maybe," Allister said. "But she was a tough old broad." He tapped lightly on the hood of the limo. "Good day to you, Mr. Vice President."

Allister shut the door to the car and walked up the steps to his home.

He had an organization to manage.

The Las Vegas sunrise was not like other sunrises. It seemed to compete with the constant neon glow of the casinos. But not today. Today, there was no power on the Strip, and so, for the first time in God knew how many years, the sunrise was as natural as it could be.

Megatron watched as his Decepticons and the Autobots slowly recovered their wits. Ratchet was helping to get them much needed energy. Optimus Prime, or whatever he was now, was nowhere to be seen. Omega Sentinel and Devastator had absorbed the impact of the nuclear fire and would need....a lot of help, Megatron thought. *They'll have to be rebuilt.*

The last Keeper, who had been Starscream and Bluestreak, was nothing more than molten metal and ash.

He considered his options. If he ordered the Decepticons to attack right now, they would likely be able to overwhelm the exhausted Autobots. Except there was Optimus Prime and the Matrix. Somewhere nearby, no doubt.

Soundwave kept looking at him furtively as did the others as if to say, "Now?," but Megatron did not give the order.

During the long night, he'd reached a better plan.

"Decepticons!" he said. "To me!"

They gathered around. "It's over," Megatron said. "We will return to base."

"But I thought—" Soundwave began, and Megatron cut him off.

"I know what you thought," Megatron said. "I have

chosen a different path for now. We will leave immediately."

"Now that Starscream is dead, who's second in command?" Skywarp asked.

"You are," Megatron said, noting with some glee the ire on Soundwave's features. It never paid to do the expected around Decepticons. "For now."

"It's the only logical thing to do," Skywarp said.

"Some might disagree," Megatron said. "But no matter. Get the pieces of Devastator and Omega Sentinel that are left. We will rebuild them."

"And that thing?" Skywarp asked, pointing to the form of the Keeper that had held both Starscream and Bluestreak.

"We'll have to...unmeld him somehow," Megatron said. "He will be rebuilt, if for no other reason than to answer for his treacheries. Leave the pieces of Bluestreak for the Autobots to deal with."

The Decepticons began gathering pieces of their fallen warriors and preparing to leave. Megatron watched them carefully. A moment's inattention could lead to disaster when you were the leader of such treacherous machines. Shortly, they were starting to head back to the Nemises, hidden deep beneath the Pacific Ocean.

He was about to give up on seeing Optimus, when the Autobot leader was found in a crater nearby. Ratchet immediately jumped in and began to help the human called Spike, who looked more dead than alive. He also looked at Optimus in regards to that horribly cheerful little car they called Bumblebee, but Optimus shook his head sadly, then climbed out of the pit. *A pity*, Megatron noted. *I'd been hoping to kill that one myself.*

He cut quite an impressive figure in that Energon-enhanced armor, Megatron thought as he noticed that Prime's armor was shifting slowly back to his original colors. If he'd stayed that way, every Decepticon would have feared him forever.

"Megatron," Optimus said. "Omega Sentinel and Devastator?"

"No," Megatron said. "We'll have to rebuild Devastator. There's too much damage to Omega Sentinel. There's nothing we can do with him."

"I suspected," he said. "I'm sorry that I wasn't able to help them more."

Megatron laughed. "You're *sorry*!"

"Yes," Optimus said. "I would've done more if I could."

"You're unbelievable," Megatron said. "Will you be rebuilding that...car?"

"I don't know if it's possible. The damage was severe. He wasn't truly built for combat." Optimus sighed. "We will try."

"I never thought he was," Megatron said.

"It's over now," Optimus said. "The Keepers are dead. At least we accomplished that much."

"I'd say you accomplished it more than any of us," Megatron said. "But there is one more thing..."

Optimus stared at his long time enemy, and Megatron sensed that he knew what was coming and was powerless to stop it.

Time to cash in my chips, Megatron thought.

EPILOGUE

Optimus Prime had known this moment would come.

On the Keepers' world, in exchange for his assistance, Megatron had wanted a favor to be named later. Optimus had agreed. At the time, there had been little choice. And now Megatron was about to call that favor in.

"But there is one more thing…" Megatron was saying.

Optimus gazed at Megatron. "Yes?" he said, fearing the worst.

"The matter of that favor you owe me."

The pure, evil glee in Megatron's voice was enough to warn Optimus that his nemesis had a plan. "I agreed to a favor," Optimus said. "I am honor bound to answer your request."

"I know," Megatron said simply. "That's what makes you so predictable."

"Perhaps," Optimus said. He kept his voice even, though his mind raced trying to figure out what the Decepticon would want.

"You are," Megatron asserted. "But that's not what we're here to talk about."

"No," Prime said. "It's not." He glanced at the Autobots who were watching this exchange with interest. "What would you have of me?"

"Nothing much really," Megatron said. "A trifle in

return for my much needed assistance on the Keepers' world."

"Out with it," Prime snarled, his patience fraying. "I have work to do."

Megatron grinned, his evil intent as clear as the sun on the horizon. He stood in front of Optimus, his face only inches away. "Very well, but remember your precious honor is at stake when you hear my request."

"I am aware of my obligations," Optimus said. "Now state your request."

"I want you to name *me* Prime." Megatron's mocking laughter rose up and into the sky.

The Matrix! Prime thought helplessly, knowing he was caught on his own promise.

If I name him Prime, he'll be able to take the Matrix and hide it away...and the odds will be very much in their favor when the battle between us is rejoined.